Copyright © 2021 Katie Berry

All rights reserved.

ASIN: B08W1SN1S9
Print ISBN-13: 979-8705198900

No portions of this book may be reproduced without permission from the publisher, except as permitted by Canadian copyright law.

Published by Fuzzy Bean Books

Cover Art Copyright © 2020 Fiona Jayde Media

This is a work of fiction. Names, characters, businesses, places, events, locales, and incidents are either the products of the author's imagination or used in a fictitious manner. Any resemblance to actual persons, living or dead, or actual events is purely coincidental.

ABANDONED
ARRIVALS AND AWAKENINGS
A
LIVELY DEADMARSH
NOVEL

BOOK 1

KATIE BERRY

For Craig Charles, may you be at peace.

ENTER TO WIN!

Visit Katieberry.ca and join my newsletter to become a Katie Berry Books Insider. By simply sharing your email address*, you will be entered into the monthly draws! That's right, draws, plural.

Each month there will be two draws, one for a free copy of CLAW: A Canadian Thriller from Audiobooks.com, and the other, a free autographed copy of CLAW: A Canadian Thriller on paperback delivered right to your mailbox. There will be other contests, chapter previews, short stories, and more coming soon, so don't miss out!

Become a Katie Berry Books Insider today at:

https://katieberry.ca/become-a-katie-berry-books-insider-and-win/

*Your email address will not be sold, traded, or given away. It will be kept strictly confidential and will only be used by Katie Berry Books to notify you of new content, contests and prize winners.

ACKNOWLEDGEMENTS

Special thanks to Paulina, Maggie, Riel, Betty, Jen, Gord, Gary, Bob, and Michael. Your support, enthusiasm and good humour has meant so much to me as I have put this story together. The insights and input that you provided have helped immensely in the crafting of this tale of dark and lonely places and I thank you most sincerely.

-Katie Berry

PREFACE

Hello, Dear Reader. Thank you for booking your stay at the Sinclair Resort Hotel. Please make sure to enjoy everything the resort has to offer. You don't want to miss a thing! If you have any concerns during your stay here, please contact the concierge service in the lobby, Katie@katieberry.ca.

All kidding aside, the novel you hold in your hands, the first of four, has been in the works for several years now. Disappearances, mass and otherwise, have always fascinated me. Growing up, I read about the usual suspects, such as Flight 19, the Mary Celeste, the Roanoke Colony, and of course, the Anjikuni Lake Incident (which is in dispute in some circles).

My mind has always run rampant with the thought of what *may* have happened at the scenes of these mysterious occurrences. And so, after a lifetime of reading fantastic fiction crafted by the likes of Jules Verne, H. G. Wells, Stephen King, Dean Koontz, Michael Crichton, and hundreds of other amazing authors, I decided it was time to tell the tale that has been floating around in my head for the last few years.

This novel is the result of those musings, and I sincerely hope you enjoy ABANDONED: A Lively Deadmarsh Novel Book 1. Stay tuned for Book 2 coming in spring of 2021.

Good health and great reads to you all,

-Katie Berry
February 19th, 2021

"Sometimes, a place is just born bad."

-Author Unknown

CHAPTER ONE

December 31st, 1981 2359 hours

Esmeralda Cruz tugged her serving cart back from the elevator doors, a brief flash of recollection making her suddenly anxious. Magnums of Dom Perignon Champagne near the cart's edge jingled musically from the sudden motion.

After what had happened here a couple of weeks ago, she now stayed well away from this elevator's doors, and thankfully, had almost forgotten as a result. And that was because part of her didn't want to remember. She shuddered, her chestnut ponytail bouncing lightly along the nape of her neck, still in disbelief about what she thought she'd seen.

The brass indicator arrow above the doors inched toward the letter 'B' on the left-hand side. She sighed and looked at her wristwatch. The second hand on her Timex was sweeping far too rapidly around the dial toward twelve. She was supposed to have this cart of refreshments to the grand ballroom before midnight, but it looked like she might be delayed by a few seconds due to waiting for the elevator. It was something she hadn't expected and had left the kitchen with very little time to make it upstairs.

With a ping, the elevator arrived. Her breath hitched in her chest as the doors slid apart. It was empty inside, or so it seemed.

A wall of arctic cold rolled from the service elevator's cramped confines to greet her, embracing her in its frigid folds. Her skin tingled, suddenly gooseflesh. The basement of this resort was usually several degrees cooler than the upper floors, but she'd never experienced anything as extreme as this. The thin fabric of her polyester serving uniform did little to protect her from this bone-chilling cold, and she released the cart handle to rub her hands up and down her arms to gain warmth.

Her heart began to pulse within her chest as she moved toward the doors, each beat feeling as if it might be her last. There were several areas inside this resort that gave her the willies — places where she hated going and avoided if she could at all costs. Number one was the grand ballroom on the main floor, number two was the royal suite on the third floor, and number three stood open just before her.

With a deep inhale, she pushed the cart into the elevator. The champagne jangled as the cart's wheels bumped across the narrow, black gap leading into the car. Her eyes were locked onto the gap, her knuckles white from the strength of her grip on the cart's handle. Always slightly panicked in tight spaces, she generally hated going inside any of the elevators at the Sinclair Hotel. But she hated going inside this particular one most of all. After what happened here last time, she'd hoped that she would never have to use this elevator again, especially at night.

It had been her first shift at the resort, and she'd been making a late evening delivery to a catered party in the royal suite. Much like tonight, not wanting to spill anything, she'd been pushing the cart ever so slowly over the small black gap between the shaft wall and the elevator car.

A faint, almost inaudible voice, suddenly came to her, whispering something over and over.

Sound carried exceptionally well along the basement's network of concrete service passageways. At first, she'd thought it had been a co-worker conversing in a low voice with someone, just out of sight, around another turn in the corridor. And yet, she hadn't seen anyone nearby on her way to the elevator.

Halfway onto the lift she heard the voice again and paused, peering out into the hallway a final time, but saw no one there. She'd continued pushing the cart inside, then glanced downward as the second set of wheels rolled with a bump across the small gap.

And then she'd screamed.

There, just for the briefest of moments near the cart's wheels, fingers appeared. The nails were raw, broken and bloody, clawing forth from the black gap as if some damned soul were seeking purgatory's escape.

Not caring if she spilled anything now, she thrust the cart the rest of the way in, turning it to fit in one panicked motion. She turned back to the door, about to shriek again, but the fingers were gone. Esmeralda was pressed back against the cold steel of the elevator car, her eyes riveted on the black gap. Had she only imagined the fingers? Leaning reluctantly toward the narrow slit, she called out in a timid voice, "Is anyone down there?"

There had been no reply, and she'd pounded the third-floor button to close the doors as quickly as she could, hoping desperately not to see the fingers reappear as the doors slowly squealed shut.

On the ride up that afternoon, she'd vowed to avoid this elevator at all costs in the future, and yet here she now stood. With a shudder, she returned to the present. There were no fingers tonight, and she was thankful for that. The lift doors slid closed with a squeal like long fingernails scraping across a chalkboard.

She shuddered again, watching her breath steam from her parted lips. Loosening her death-grip on the cart handle, she jabbed the lobby call button several times with her thumb, trying to hasten her trip to the main floor. With each hand crossed to the opposing arm, she rubbed herself, trying to keep warm. After a moment, the lift's ancient electric motor kicked in, and it began raising her to ground level.

For whatever reason, this hotel was cold in the strangest of places, but not consistently so. The cold spots had a habit of coming and going. One day she would feel a chill while working in a particular part of the hotel, but other days she'd be back to the same spot and not feel it at all. There seemed to be no rhyme nor reason to it. But she'd never experienced a cold like this in any other areas inside the hotel before, except perhaps the kitchen's walk-in freezer.

She wrinkled her nose slightly at the serving cart's other occupants. Chilled mounds of beluga caviar, flaky snow crab meat and piles of jumbo shrimp glistened in the elevator's dim light. Esmeralda was eager to deliver this aromatic cargo to its final destination, the smorgasbord in the main ballroom. Though she envied the people who would soon partake of this repast, she was more preoccupied with thoughts of her own late-night dinner date with the handsome new maintenance man she'd just met last week.

A cheer went up, and with loud fanfare, Baby New Year 1982 toddled onto the scene. The first, bass-heavy blasts of Auld Lang Syne bounced down from the ballroom above, courtesy of the swing-pop band, the Glenn Millers. She began humming along with the music.

Sudden darkness consumed her world, and the elevator lurched to a squealing stop. Esmeralda held her breath for a moment, waiting. A loud click came from the ceiling above, and the emergency power came on. Behind yellow glass, an ageing bulb struggled to light. It buzzed for a moment, brightening to an almost eye-shielding level of brightness, and then it dimmed to the colour of concentrated urine, doing little to dispel the gloom inside the small space. Esmeralda let out another breath she didn't realise she was holding, and it plumed from her mouth like she'd just exhaled after taking a puff on a cigarette.

The resort had been suffering electrical blackouts over the last few weeks, starting just before Esmeralda began her employment at the Sinclair. She'd bumped into Elmer from electrical maintenance the other day, and he'd told her he'd been looking into the problem, but obviously, he'd yet to solve it. She never knew when the resort would be plunged once more into blackness.

Trying to reassure herself, she was about to begin humming along with the music when she realised there was none. At the Christmas eve gala last week, another blackout had occurred at a banquet and dance she'd been working. There'd been the expected murmurs of discontent when it went dark, but it had all been accompanied by the continuing music of the band as they played.

Tonight, she strained to hear anything, any sound at all, but there was nothing — no music or drunken shouts of dismay at the unexpected darkness, absolutely nothing. The musicians working the event at the last outage were the same ones as tonight. That time, they'd continued to play until the power came back on. It made sense they would do so since most of that band was not on any sort of electric amplifier, except the keyboard and bass player. Plus, the music had kept the partygoers relatively calm. But not tonight; tonight was different. The music had just ended, suddenly turned off like a radio in mid-tune as if the band had never really been there in the first place. It was quiet as a morgue above her head.

The fluorescent light panel overhead suddenly flickered back on, and the lift groaned to life. The crystal on Esmeralda's Timex wristwatch revealed that she'd only been in the semi-dark for about fifteen seconds. She was more than relieved when the doors finally pinged open on the main floor. She stepped out, rolling the cart before her. Breathing deeply, she enjoyed the stale and slightly musty, but gloriously unconfined air of the rear service passageway. And thankfully, it was much warmer up here as well, the bone-chilling cold now gone.

Esmeralda was still getting to know her way around the place. Hired for a room service attendant/bus girl position, she was almost always in awe of the majestic old hotel's beautiful decor around her as she went about her delivery duties. On several occasions, she'd found herself getting lost within the intricate maze of corridors and rooms that comprised the interior of the massive old brick and stone building. Sometimes, as she made her room service drops, the corridors didn't lead to where she thought they should, and on more than one occasion found herself at a dead end. But other times, she would come out in a completely different part of the hotel than she'd expected. It seemed as if the corridors changed direction as she pushed her cart through them, turning her around on purpose. She knew that wasn't possible, however, and figured it was just another example of her poor sense of direction.

Thankfully, this evening, she had been spared all of room service's mindless mundanities. Tonight, she was serving the West Coast's best and brightest writers, directors, and actors, as well as their significant others — the TV people, as she called them. They were all attending an award show and dinner-dance at the resort to celebrate the new year as well as the accomplishments of the West Coast's burgeoning television and film industry. It was an annual thing, running at the hotel since it had first been chosen as the site for the award show back in 1963.

She'd been amazed to learn one of her favourite shows, The Littlest Hobo, was filmed by some of the beautiful people in the ballroom. She smiled as she thought of the television show, and the magnificent dog that starred in it, as well as that American show with the other equally amazing dog, Lassie. Those were two programmes of which she tried not to miss a single episode, whenever she had a chance to watch the TV.

Despite having to work on such a romantic evening of the year, Esmeralda really didn't mind, since she would soon be spending a romantic late-night dinner date with Fernando from maintenance. They had met while going about their duties at the resort. After pushing her room service cart down yet another wrong corridor, Esmeralda had been in the process of turning around and he'd just been there, behind her in the passage all of a sudden like he'd materialised out of thin air. She'd let out a small squeak of fright and automatically apologised through force of habit in Spanish.

When the handsome maintenance man replied in her native tongue, she'd been surprised. After some kind words to melt her heart, he'd asked her out on a date for New Year's Eve after her shift, and she'd said yes. She felt quite flattered that such a good-looking young man was interested in her. Esmeralda's English was quite good, but it was always nice to have a native speaker of her home language around to talk to when she felt homesick. Plus, Fernando was incredibly easy on the eyes as well, more handsome than any other man she remembered seeing in her brief nineteen years on the planet. He should be a star with his dark hair, deep-blue eyes, and straight white teeth. In fact, he was so good looking, she thought he should be inside the room attending the ball with the TV people as well.

All of these thoughts and more were swirling through Esmeralda's head as she wheeled the cart along the passageway toward the rear entrance of the grand ballroom. The absence of any sound soon came back to haunt her, and she felt a chill scuttle along the nape of her neck as all thoughts of joy and pleasure disappeared.

Pushing the cart through the rear service door into the back of the ballroom, Esmeralda's first thought was that she must have entered the wrong room by mistake. Perhaps she'd gotten a bit turned around, lost as she was with thoughts of Fernando at the forefront of her mind as he so often was these days. There were three ballrooms at the Sinclair Hotel, but only one of them was in use this evening, and that was the grand ballroom. She backed up through the doors, meaning to look at the room number, thinking that surely she must have gotten confused.

A deep, rumbling voice at her back gave her a start. "Esmeralda! What do you think you're doing? Watch where you're going!" Leonard Hunter, the kitchen and banquet manager for the evening, crowded into the open doorway behind her, agitatedly trying to peer through.

With a shriek, Esmeralda jolted as if electrified, her hands spasming briefly, the frosty bottles of champagne threatening to topple over. She turned to Hunter and said with a tremor, "I'm so sorry, sir! I thought I was in the wrong ballroom and wanted to double-check the number."

"Why? What's the matter?" he asked, straining to see past her, eager to get into the room to make sure the guests were not in too much distress after the power outage.

"Something's wrong in there," Esmeralda said in a hushed voice. As she finished talking, she saw that Leonard Hunter was already looking over her petite brown head into the room beyond, his mouth now hanging agape. She turned back toward the room, her eyes wide and unblinking.

Enormous chandeliers sparkled from the hammered copper ceiling high overhead. Red and gold bunting flowed along the walls like shining satin rivers. Along one wall, a long table bedecked in colour-coordinated fabric offered a full midnight smorgasbord with seemingly every delicacy a person could imagine. Across from it, a massive 'Happy New Year 1982' banner ran the length of the room near the ceiling, dangling over the tops of dozens of high windows. Outside, gusting snow scraped along the window-glass on crystalline claws, and the wind howled as if a beast possessed, trying to get inside.

They strained to hear any sound coming from within the room; a laugh or giggle perhaps, or maybe a drunken New Year's kiss being stolen in a corner somewhere. But there was nothing, and silence now held reign.

The dance floor was littered with balloons and streamers that had fallen from netting overhead, released when the clock had struck midnight. They lay undisturbed in a circular pattern on the floor underneath the netting, with no sign of anyone having danced through them after they'd fallen.

Full drinks sat next to plates stacked high with sweet and savoury delicacies. Cigarettes and cigars burned away in the heavy crystal ashtrays, with minimal ash dangling from their tips, looking as if freshly lit, ready for their respective owners to take their next drag.

Esmeralda Cruz glanced back over her shoulder at Leonard Hunter. Their gazes locked for a brief moment. In his eyes, she could see he was struggling with the same things she felt inside — confusion, disbelief, and utter terror.

There was no sound to be heard inside the vast room because there was no longer any living soul inside of it to make any noise.

At the stroke of midnight, December 31st, 1981, ninety-eight beautiful people vanished without a trace from the grand ballroom of the Sinclair Resort Hotel, never to be seen or heard from again.

CHAPTER TWO

December 23rd, 2021 1831 hours

The highway wound back upon itself at every serpentine curve, coiling and caressing the cloud-shrouded mountains, the sun only a dim memory as the winter storm smothered the remaining life from the cold, December afternoon.

A heavy layer of fresh snow covered the road. Lively Deadmarsh drove the hazardous highway with a skill honed from years of experience, giving him a confident ability that he might not have otherwise possessed, growing up, as he had, in the mild winter rains that seemed trademark to Vancouver, British Columbia.

According to the gauge on the dashboard, the temperature had dropped another four degrees over the last three treacherous kilometres. The higher he went, the worse it got, making what had started out as a damp, showery afternoon at Vancouver's harbour-front helipad, into a snowy, miserable winter's evening higher up in the mountains.

The SUV's heated, leather-wrapped steering wheel and seats kept Lively more than comfortable. But perhaps a little too cosy, in fact, as he'd felt himself on the verge of drowsing off as he piloted the Toyota 4Runner into the storm.

Leaning to the right, Lively elbowed open a cooler on the seat next to him. He extracted a can of Barq's Root Beer with his right hand. Bracing it between his legs, he cracked the can open. The cold liquid hit the back of his throat, coating it with a burbling blend of caffeine and sugar. Though the soda kept him somewhat alert behind the wheel, it also had the unfortunate effect of filling his already full bladder to almost bursting.

Propped up on the dashboard, his cell phone displayed a map of his current location. "Okay, Emily." The phone's artificial intelligence system beeped, confirming its undivided attention to his upcoming request. "Find the closest restroom."

After a moment, the map program did its search, and a smooth, slightly robotic female voice came out of the 4Runner's speaker system, "There is a provincial rest stop five minutes ahead. Would you like to set a temporary waypoint?"

"Yes, I would."

"Waypoint set."

"Gracias, Emily."

"De nada," the cell phone replied.

Surprised to receive a response to his expression of gratitude, in Spanish no less, he smiled. He was amazed by the new capabilities and human-style interactions constantly being added to cell phones and other devices — some days he truly felt like he was living in the future.

Lively drove in silence for the next few minutes, squinting through the windshield at the storm currently battering the four-wheel drive. Wind-driven ice crystals scoured across the windshield like a sandstorm with some of the gusts threatening to tear the steering wheel from his hand. After several tense seconds however, the wind died down for a moment and snowflakes as big as salad plates began to surge hypnotically past the SUV's high-intensity headlights, making it look for all the world like he'd somehow managed to bump the 4Runner's speed to warp factor one. Moments later, the illusion was shattered when another huge gust of wind came along and shredded the delicate latticework of large flakes, rending them to ice crystals and raking them across the windshield once more.

"Your destination is on the right," Emily chimed. With a sigh of relief, Lively spied the rest stop, barely visible due to snow blanketing most of the blue and white rectangular sign.

Feeling as if his kidneys were preparing to high-five his bladder in excitement, Lively slowed the Toyota to a crawl, starting to pull in, but stopped when he saw a two-metre-high snowdrift blocking the rest stop's unplowed entrance. He frowned through the passenger-side window at the happy stick people camping beside their stick tents and picnic tables. A small sign was plastered diagonally across the bottom proclaiming the rest stop to be 'Closed for the Season'. Some smart-ass with a can of spray paint had added, 'Reason? Freezin!'.

"Well, you got that part right, my friend." Lively said, looking glumly at the graffiti on the sign. He put the 4Runner back in gear and pulled out onto the highway, shaking his head. He was getting close to just stepping out of the SUV and letting things fly, but some internal sense of propriety held him back from doing so. Well, if worse came to worst, he reasoned, he would just have to emulate a trucker and 'check his brakes' in another few kilometres. "That's just lovely, isn't it, Emily? No rest for my bladder at this stop," he commented, shaking his head.

Hearing its name mentioned, his cell phone's always-listening AI responded, "The next nearest rest stop is located thirty kilometres away in Entwistle, British Columbia. You are now approximately fifteen minutes from your current destination of Overseer Mountain. Would you like to change destinations and plot a new course back to Entwistle?"

The snowfall outside of the windshield was almost horizontal now that the wind had kicked up again, and Lively knew that Emily's estimate was lollipops and rainbows time. It would actually be much longer since it was nearing whiteout conditions on the road and it slowed his progress to a crawl. But he also knew he had no choice and responded, "Cancel, Emily."

"No problem, your original destination is still set."

A flash of headlights up ahead suddenly informed him he was not the only person stupid enough to be out on the roads tonight. A couple of seconds later, a snowplow blasted by, kicking up a snowstorm of its own. He reconsidered his thought — that guy wasn't stupid; he was getting paid to be out here. "Rather them, than me", he muttered, turning up the heat a bit more as he watched the snowplows' taillights dwindle to twin red specks in his rear-view mirror. He smiled suddenly, thinking that he, too, was getting paid to be out here. But Lively's job wasn't one for the public's safety; instead, it was to try and shed new light on a mystery more disturbing than anything he'd ever encountered so far in his career. Amazing what one does for money, he mused.

The road up to the resort was private and like the hotel, had been closed to the public since the incident had occurred in order to keep the looky loos of the world at bay. At least it seemed that whoever controlled things regarding maintenance at the resort was keeping the road clear for their arrival. Lively didn't know what it would cost to have a private firm plowing a thirty kilometre stretch of road like this. Probably more than the twenty bucks he remembered charging as a boy when he would shovel his neighbour's laneways during Vancouver's single, annual snowstorm that hit each winter.

Unfortunately, that storm was what the West Coast had been experiencing for the last forty-eight hours now, and it was a doozy, battering the coast for two days straight so far. He squinted intently through the windshield, willing his overfull bladder to hang in there for the next little while and not make him a candidate for Depends Undergarments as he crawled the SUV toward the resort. Despite the road being recently plowed, it was still slow going due to the limited visibility.

Lively was not a winter person. He liked to avoid the worst that winter had to offer in Canada, especially nights like this, having grown up and lived most of his life on the rainy West Coast. Somehow, the thought of freezing to death in the mountains on his way to an abandoned resort didn't seem particularly appealing, and although he drove with confidence, he also drove with caution.

This afternoon he'd choppered in from three-hundred kilometres out at sea. What had started out as a relaxing vacation had devolved into something else entirely when his ship picked up something while at sea in the middle of the cruise. And this something had not been a flu virus or food poisoning, there was no question of that. However, it had been deadly, and the surviving passengers and crew ended up with a vacation experience they would not soon forget. He'd hailed a taxi to his condo and grabbed his

Toyota 4Runner from the garage. Everything that he might need for his trip to the Sinclair had been packed into the SUV before departing for his cruise. Not a man to leave anything to the last minute, he usually tried to go wherever he was going, prepared.

And now here he was on his way to this new case. But calling it 'new' was a bit of a misnomer. Although he was opening a fresh investigation into the Sinclair Incident through his personal investigative agency, what had happened up there was definitely not new. The Sinclair Resort, high in the mountains of Western Canada, had long fascinated millions of people around the world. It was an event that left everyone questioning their own reality as they tried to understand what had occurred that bizarre evening.

One such group still trying to understand was the holding company that had taken over the resort just after the event occurred. A couple of weeks before the cruise, a bulky document had arrived by registered mail. For whatever reason, the holding company had requested Lively's assistance in helping 'restore' the resort and make it available to the public again. Multi-use scenarios were bandied about in the letter, from a refurbished hotel and condos to an outright tourist attraction based on the mysterious disappearance.

Of course, by the word 'restore', he knew they actually meant that they wanted him to help 'cure' the place of whatever malignancy had taken it over. The fate of the people in the ballroom was now legendary and filled with as much speculation as that of the first Roanoke Colony. And like any company, if some money could be made from their investment after all these years, then they were going to try and collect on it.

Since the building had been tightly sealed after the bankruptcy, not much was known of the interior's condition. Now, after forty years, the company wanted to know once and for all if it was safe for anyone to set foot in the door. Lively had been chosen to be that someone and he'd accepted in a heartbeat, no questions asked. It wasn't really a hard choice for him, seeing as the incident was his own personal Holy Grail of unexplained happenings since early childhood. And a nice bonus had been the retainer cheque for an ungodly amount of money that they'd included with the query letter. Ultimately, it all added up to something to which he could not say no.

In the intervening weeks, while he'd been 'relaxing' on his cruise, Lively had been able to do quite a bit of research on the Sinclair. He'd requested and, surprisingly, received copies of the police reports from the lead RCMP investigator at the time, Chief Inspector John Harder. Also included were interviews of guests and staff who had reported strange happenings before and after the event. Lively had taken some of his holiday time to compile all of this material into a journal. All in all, he had almost three-hundred pages of information about that snowy December evening four decades ago when the power went out.

Lively snapped out of his reverie as the SUV's tires temporarily lost traction. The rear end of the vehicle began to fishtail, and his winter driving skills kicked in automatically. In one smooth adrenalised motion, he turned the wheel in the direction of the skid, bringing the vehicle quickly back under control. He was a confident driver, thanks to hundreds of hours of training, including extensive, in-the-field experience with defensive and offensive driving techniques. Of all the courses he'd taken over the years, extreme winter driving was his favourite.

"Well, I gotta say, that shot of adrenaline perked me up more than the Barq's did." But now, suddenly thinking of fluids again, Lively found the jiggling movement of the SUV made his full bladder chatter even more insistently. But despite this need to pee, he pressed on through the driving snow, but took it slow — there was no other way to go.

He was in no hurry to meet any of the other parties involved in the case at this point since there was no one else to meet. After the disappearance, the entire resort had been temporarily shut down as an open crime scene in order that the investigation could proceed unhindered. But what was supposed to have been a short closure turned into weeks, which stretched into months and finally dragged into years. No further reservations were taken after the incident, and the hotel never reopened, finally declaring bankruptcy in 1985 after the massive payout incurred from the lawsuit settlement.

For almost four decades now, no one had entered the building, and it had remained untouched. Whatever walked the darkened hallways of the Sinclair Resort Hotel since then, had walked alone.

CHAPTER THREE

January 1st, 1982 0602 hours

Inspector John Harder of the Royal Canadian Mounted Police thought he'd seen it all. He'd been involved in several missing person cases over the years, including a possible murder-suicide up here at the Sinclair many years before, but he'd never had a case where so many people had just disappeared all at once.

He'd been awakened at 12:30 A.M. by the insistent ringing of the phone next to his bed. Not being ones to stay up late, he and Helen had turned in early last night. Despite the magical night and all of its lovely romantic connotations, after being married for twenty-five years, they were both content just to be together and found themselves napping side by side in their chairs by nine.

So now, here he was, only six hours into the new year with less than two hours of sleep, overseeing an investigation that might turn out to be one of the biggest mass disappearances in modern history.

As he surveyed the interior of the grand ballroom, he was reminded of the Mary Celeste. That ship was found adrift at sea with all hands and all passengers missing. When boarded, nothing was found disturbed or out of place. It was as if everyone on board had vanished right in the middle of whatever they were doing. The galley had dinner laid out for everyone, with bowls of soup and cups of coffee still warm to the touch. There were no signs of violence or struggle, which seemed to rule out pirates. Had that been the case, the ship would have shown some signs of looting or disturbance, but there was nothing.

It was the same here at the Sinclair: flutes of champagne sat full and untouched, cigarettes and cigars in ashtrays were burnt down to stubs as if they'd all been lit by their owners and then completely forgotten afterwards. The smorgasbord was still laid out on its table, growing cold and dry. John hadn't wanted anything removed; he'd mandated that food, table settings and drinks stay where they were until samples could be taken of everything.

Scratching his head, Harder smiled ruefully. He'd just finished interviewing the first people to arrive on the scene, a young Hispanic woman and her supervisor. As of right now, he knew as much as they did, which was just about nothing. The young woman, one Esmeralda Cruz, had arrived just moments before her supervisor, and neither had seen anyone in the corridor departing the room as they approached. In fact, the woman recalled hearing the band playing music as she rode up in the elevator from the basement. When the power had gone out halfway through the journey, the music stopped, which she said she found strange. Once the power came back on, she'd hoped the band would start playing again, but they never did.

Her supervisor, Leonard Hunter, had come hustling up the stairwell from the basement-level kitchen, wanting to make sure that everything was running smoothly.

Harder asked the manager why there were no other staff in the ballroom before the occurrence. Hunter had been evasive at first, but when John pressed him further, the man had admitted to allowing some of the staff to start their New Years early and have a few drinks down in the kitchen. He admitted to feeling both ashamed and relieved that the rest of the staff was not in the ballroom when the incident occurred, thanks to his impromptu staff party.

John shook his head. All told, there were ninety-eight people in that room, plus nine band members — all now gone. It was as if they had been erased from existence. How had that many people disappeared in the short space of fifteen seconds? It wouldn't have been long enough to get even half of that many through the emergency doors for a fire drill. Maybe in a full minute, but not fifteen seconds.

Small wisps of vapour plumed from Harder's mouth, and he shivered both from the cold and the unknown. There seemed to be a chill in the ballroom that no amount of fiddling with the thermostat for the electric baseboard heat could fix. It was like someone had left the emergency doors open for several hours to air the room out even though the temperature outside was well into the minus twenties.

He moved slowly toward the centre of the massive ballroom. Snaking across the floor, a psychedelic flower made of multi-coloured balloon petals blossomed at his feet, with red and gold streamers intertwining like stems. A spider's web of netting dangled overhead, looking to have previously held the balloons and streamers before their midnight release.

These items should have been disturbed where people had danced through the colourful potpourri as it fell. However, that didn't seem to be the case here. It looked like when they were dropped, everyone was already gone from the room by the time they hit the ground. But how could that be? Did the entire ballroom decide to go for a stroll into oblivion all at once? All at the stroke of midnight with a speed not humanly possible? He figured if there were a giant trap door in the floor, everything would be gone inside this room, and not just the people. So, he ruled that out fairly quickly.

And then there was the fact that there were no footprints near the ballroom's emergency exits or anywhere else outside, except for a single set left by the bartender near one door. The snow lay pristine and untouched, sparkling weakly in the early-morning sunlight just now spilling over snow-capped peaks in the distance. The storm had broken just after midnight, and a new cold front now blanketed the area, freezing everything solid.

A tentative knock came at Harder's back, and he turned. Peering meekly into the ballroom, a young female constable, Jansen, informed him that a message was waiting for him at the front desk.

John had been initially reluctant to leave the ballroom and lose his train of thought, but upon entering the lobby, he was pleased and mystified to note how much warmer it was in this part of the hotel. He retrieved the message from the front desk night manager and scanned it quickly. The forensics team wouldn't arrive for another two hours due to an equipment delay. He sighed.

Night desk manager Arthur Baldwin adjusted his tie. Heavyset, sallow and pale, it seemed that he was not on speaking terms with sunlight and exercise. He stood shadowed in the alcove leading to the darkened office at his back, touching his hand to the side of his face.

Sometimes, Harder liked to have multiple interviews of the same witness done by different officers. This was one of those times and the night manager was one of those witnesses. He decided to have Baldwin go over things with him while he waited for forensics to arrive. John pulled a microcassette recorder from his pocket, along with a notebook and pencil. "I know you already spoke with Corporal Jansen, but if you could also tell me what happened, Mr. Baldwin, it would be appreciated."

Baldwin gently rubbed at the side of his shadow-cloaked face for another moment, then cleared his throat. "Sure, why not. It's pretty much burned into my memory, now." With a deep sigh and another pause to adjust his glasses, he began.

"It can be kind of quiet around here sometimes, New Year's Eve being no exception. Let me tell you, I know that from experience. I've been here for a while now, since just after the other night guy disappeared, or got murdered or whatever happened to him. So, it's good to have a book to read or something to watch on TV." Baldwin trailed off, over his shoulder into the darkened office briefly as if he'd heard something, his face still partially obscured in shadow. "I was just about to sit down for a few minutes to check out the beginning of the late show, to see if it was going to be any good, you know?"

Harder nodded encouragingly.

"Then, the power went out, and the first thing I thought to myself was, 'Oh great, here we go again!' Last week, I was swamped at the desk when the power had gone out for half a minute. And I figured that it might be a problem this time as well because of the group in the ballroom. So, I was kind of surprised."

"Surprised? By what?"

"How nobody came to complain. By the time I was done fumbling under the front desk for the flashlight, I had thought I'd see at least one or two of them storming toward me. I can see down the corridor leading to the ballrooms from here, but there was no one approaching." Baldwin hesitated for a moment, as if unsure he should continue and say what he was going to say, then blurted, "And then some weird shit happened."

Yes, Harder thought, weird shit indeed. In fact, today was definitely a shoo-in for 'Weirdest Shit of 1982', even though they were only six hours into this new year. With a grunt, he said instead, "Please go ahead, Mr. Baldwin."

"So, anyway, the emergency lights kicked in about five seconds after the power went off, just like they usually do. And I know that they're normally quite dim, but it was kinda strange."

"How so?"

"Well, just before I located the flashlight, I heard this pounding. I wasn't sure what it was at first. Thought maybe it was the drummer going crazy in the ballroom or something. Then I realised it sounded more like some really big guy running down the stairs from the upper floors at full tilt, in the dark. Once I'd found the flashlight and shone it down the hallway, I figured I'd spot whoever had come down the stairs since I hadn't seen them in the lobby. But there was no one in sight. However, the strangest thing had to be the lights."

"Strange? How so?"

"So, get this: the emergency lights along the corridor dimmed and brightened all in a series, like a pulse, but just the one time, sort of like a runway at the airport. When I started making my way down there, I had to shake the flashlight a couple of times as I went cause it seemed like it was going to die on me for a second like the lights did."

"And what happened?

"First of all, there was the cold. I felt it when I was about a dozen yards from the door. So, now, of course, I figured the heat was also malfunctioning, and I thought it was going to be one of those shifts. In retrospect, I really wish it had been." He shook his head sadly.

"Please continue."

"I was expecting to hear laughter or shouting as I approached the door, or maybe music from the guys in the band that weren't electric. Playing something to soothe the savage partygoers, so to speak." He laughed tiredly.

"And was that the 'weird shit' you spoke of?"

"That certainly was strange, let me tell you, but the scary, weird shit actually happened when I opened the ballroom door." Baldwin paused again, seeming unwilling or unable to express what he'd seen.

"Go on," John said reassuringly. "I need to know what you saw."

"So, when I opened the door... There was nothing."

"Nothing? You mean it was dark in the room?" Harder asked, trying to clarify.

"No, it was more than dark." After a brief pause, he said again, "There was nothing." Baldwin rubbed the side of his face for a moment.

"More than dark? Nothing? What do you mean?"

"I mean, there was a complete absence of light in the room! It was like I was looking into outer space, here inside the hotel. The darkness just went on and on forever, into infinity." Baldwin paused, collecting his thoughts. "I've wandered through that room a few times at night when it wasn't in use." He stopped.

"And?"

"And I know I should be able to see something inside the room even if the drapes are closed, especially this time of year with all the snow outside making it a little brighter at night. I thought I should have seen a little light leaking through the gaps in the drapes, you know? And besides, the emergency lights should have kicked on inside there since they were already on out in the hallway. Maybe they were having battery issues like the weird shit that happened with the hallway emergency lights, right? But then..." Baldwin trailed off.

"Please continue, Mr. Baldwin. Anything you know may be of vital importance in this case."

"I stuck my head through the door and then I felt the real cold hit my face."

"Yes, I noticed it myself when I was in the ballroom just now."

"No, nothing like that. This was much, much colder than it feels in there now." He paused for a moment, then asked, "Did you ever use liquid nitrogen in science class back in high school?"

Harder nodded.

"So, I stuck my face into the gap between the doors to peek inside. And then I felt this searing cold, almost like I'd opened a canister of liquid nitrogen and stuck my face into it."

"Searing cold?"

"Yeah, you know, when something's so cold it feels like you're being burned. And this was the same kind of thing, but much, much, colder. Almost like I was getting frostbite instantly. Anyway, I pulled back and slammed the door shut. But not before I got this."

Harder looked up from his notepad. "Got what?"

Stepping forward from the shadows, Baldwin turned to face the inspector, the side of his face now visible. Painful-looking reddened skin covered part of Baldwin's face around his right eye and cheek as if he'd been out for a stroll in an Antarctic gale without his parka and balaclava properly adjusted. He reached up to touch it again, saying, "I only had my face in the gap for less than a second, before I slammed the door shut thinking I'd gone crazy."

Harder studied the man's face. What had happened to him in there? How did this man manage to get windburn inside a heated ballroom?

Baldwin continued, saying, "I didn't know this had happened until later, actually." He gently touched his face again. "So, anyway, I tried again after a couple of seconds, just to see."

"Just to see what?"

"To see if I actually was crazy. So, I pulled open the door open a crack again, and this time there was no black void — just the ballroom again, and the lights are coming back on inside as well. And then I see it's empty, and I'm like, what the hell? Where did everyone go? Across the room, one of the new room service girls and the kitchen manager were staring back at me. Let me tell you, they both looked as terrified and confused as I felt."

"Was there anything else, Mr. Baldwin?"

The night manager touched his hand gently to the reddened half of his face and stepped back into the darkened office, adding, "Only to say that like everything else at this resort, you've gotta be careful — it just might bite."

CHAPTER FOUR

December 23rd, 2021 1950 hours

Lively was getting close to shutting things down for the night. The snow was getting so heavy, he could barely keep the windshield clear, despite the heavy-duty winter wiper blades of the SUV. The defroster was running full tilt, but the buildup of snow on the windshield was so rapid that it laboured to keep up and the windows were threatening to fog-up completely. He shook his head ruefully, ready to pull over and nap for a few hours until the storm abated.

Emily's voice suddenly chimed from the speaker system, saying "You have arrived at your destination."

Squinting through the windshield, Lively said, "Really? Where is it?" He slowed the vehicle on the road and then stopped altogether. There was no further response from the GPS system, not that he'd been expecting one. With the elbow of his leather bomber jacket, he rubbed the passenger side window-glass, making a viewing portal for himself.

"Aha! There you are." Inset from the road by about a dozen metres, the gate to the resort was barely visible, partially buried by blowing snow — not easy to see in the dark. With a shake of his head, Lively added, "You're certainly not the easiest to find. That can't be good for the tourist trade." He hadn't seen it at first because it literally looked just like a wall of snow, with all of the whiteness blowing and swirling around it. If it hadn't been for the GPS, he would have driven right on by.

Lively cranked the wheel and pulled off the highway. He placed the 4Runner into park, its headlights illuminating the Sinclair's main gates, currently sitting closed. There was no sign of them opening automatically, and he sighed, wondering if they were unlocked. He really didn't want to go out into the cold to check, but knew he had no choice.

In the centre of the gates, wind had scoured the ground bare, creating a chest-high drift along the right-hand side. Fortunately, the left wasn't as heavily buried, its drift only knee-high, but he wasn't holding out much hope of an easy entry into the resort. If the gates didn't open, he wasn't sure if he wanted to try and scale them to gain entry right now. He might just stay in the 4Runner for the night instead. Then, when first light hit, he'd see what his options were. It wasn't worth a case of exposure to try and walk the half-mile or so from these gates to the main building, especially in light of the current storm. Had it not been blizzarding out, he may very well have attempted it – but tonight, he wasn't sure if he'd even survive the journey. The temperature gauge said it was currently twenty-five below zero outside, and it had to be twice that with the windchill. But now, here he sat, in his toasty, warm vehicle, thinking of all the frozen water outside, and his need to urinate came back with a vengeance. He realised he was going to have to admit defeat and find a tree somewhere near the side of the gate. Once he'd tended to business, he'd see if he could gain access to the property.

The moment he stepped out of the SUV, he instantly regretted it. The fierce wind lashed his legs, biting into the thin fabric of his casual cotton pants. Snow scraped along his face, and he could taste its cold brutality. He hadn't taken the time to change at his condo, he was still wearing the same clothes he'd worn on the cruise. The warmest thing he had on was his leather bomber, but its lining was not the thickest. His more seasonal clothes were in his duffle bag in the rear of the SUV. He shook his head, realising with literal cold irony that three seconds outside in this blowing snow was better than three cans of Barq's to keep a person awake and alert. However, it also exacerbated his need to go make yellow snow somewhere.

Though he was in the middle of a blizzard at the side of the road, he didn't feel he should just 'whip it out' here and take a leak on the gates of this place. It would be somewhat disrespectful, he figured. Many people viewed this site with near-religious reverence, possibly because it could be the last resting place of over one hundred victims of an, as of yet, unexplained mass murder. Those thoughts percolated through Lively's caffeinated brain as he moved to the left side of the entrance and stood facing away from the road, next to where the gate abutted a high wall when open.

A massive gust of wind tore through the entryway, and the heavy gate on the left was finally rattled loose from the confines of drifting snow leaning against it. The entrance was slightly sloped to aid in drainage during the rainy season, and it angled away to gutters on either side. Gravity helped the liberated gate, and it began moving like a locomotive down the short slope.

Lively finished his business with a small sigh and was beginning to fumble for his fly. From the corner of one eye, he caught the blur of the cast iron gate rolling rapidly toward him. He threw himself backward into the snow. With a crash, the heavy gate slammed into the stone wall where he'd been standing and bounced back several feet. Feeling slightly shaken, Lively stood upright, slowly zipping his trousers. As he dusted the snow from his legs and jacket, he said, "I guess that concludes the rest break."

When the heavy iron gate had struck the wall, most of the ice and snow had tumbled from the foot-high bronze letters affixed to its top. The first half of the resort's name was now exposed to the night's savage fury.

Many times, over the years, Lively Deadmarsh had stared evil in the face, but never so literally as tonight. 'SIN' stood only inches from his eyes, clanging against the wall in the gusting wind. The opposite gate, containing the 'CLAIR', only moved ever so slightly, still frozen in place thanks to the high drift that covered most of it.

This seemed an appropriately ominous start to this newest case, Lively thought. He'd expected it to be difficult, and perhaps one of the most dangerous he'd taken on since resigning from the Canadian Security Intelligence Service. Rarely staying at his apartment in Vancouver, he'd been hopping from one investigation to the next since CSIS. And now that he thought about it, that had actually been his life when he worked in the Service as well, so really, nothing much had changed. In fact, just before this case came across his virtual desk, he'd been tying up some loose ends and had been planning on going to Nova Scotia after his cruise to check out an aquatically named hotel which contained one very disturbing room. However, he'd put that on hold so that he could be here instead, with an entire resort hotel full of disturbing things, including one of the most infamous disappearances on the planet.

Lively climbed into the SUV with a grunt and sat with his legs facing out. To the glowing map screen of his waiting cell phone, he said, "You know, nothing starts off an investigation quite like almost getting crushed while freezing your cojones off in a snowstorm." After a pause, he added with a small smile, "Then again, it's stuff like this that gets me out of bed in the morning, isn't that right, Emily?" The AI remained mute, declining to comment on the veracity of his observation.

The heater inside the 4Runner was running full bore, just like he'd left it. A contented sigh escaped Lively's lips as his butt cheeks reaffirmed their continuing friendship with the heated leather seat. He slapped the remaining snow off of his shoes and pant legs with his gloved hands before bringing his legs all the way into the cab. He didn't particularly relish the thought of walking around the resort with wet pants for the next several hours while he got settled in.

But even slightly damp, at least he wouldn't be freezing up here tonight since the electricity was supposedly still on at the resort. According to his information, the resort had remained connected to its own personal power grid for the last forty years, thanks to some forward-thinking on the part of wealthy venture capitalist, Thomas Sinclair.

Before construction, the business magnate had ensured a steady supply of electricity would make it to his mountaintop retreat and its high-paying guests. Sinclair had been the driving force behind having a hydroelectric dam constructed at the base of Overseer Mountain outside the small town of Entwistle, BC. Some of its design was supposedly based on that of Nikola Tesla's early work in New York. Sinclair had been a lifelong fan of the man, who was an immigrant, like himself.

Thomas Sinclair's fascination with all things electrical continued and he'd made sure the entire resort was powered by his dam. And that had included the use of electric heat, as opposed to the traditional boiler and radiators popular at the time for such large structures. After the original investigation had stagnated, the hotel had been boarded up. Hopefully, it was still warm and dry inside as well. He figured that due to its castle-based origins, the building's solidity probably helped greatly in repelling the elements for all these decades.

When it opened in 1946, The Sinclair Resort Hotel had played host to a glittering panoply of stars, royalty, and the odd figure from the criminal underworld. Touted as the crown jewel of the Pacific Rim Countries, the hotel had been deemed worthy of the world's elite. As a getaway from the incessant pressures of fame and fortune, the resort had been wildly successful. Never developed as a ski hill, the local mountains surrounding the property were far too steep, their jagged grey peaks constantly battered by biting wind and sweeping storms. Instead, it had been designed as a place where one could kick back and relax, the outside world kept safely at bay on the other side of the resort's exclusive gates.

Inevitably, some of the people doing the getting away had an issue with drugs, alcohol, or both, which unfortunately created problems that needed to be cleaned up quickly. Lively had read quite extensively on this resort, trying to understand if there was something in the hotel's history that had somehow influenced what had happened in 1981.

Unlike the main highway, the laneway leading up to the resort appeared currently unplowed, with at least a foot and a half of fresh snow covering it. Putting the 4Runner in low gear, Lively started up the lane toward the resort, the SUV gaining easy purchase thanks to a set of studs installed in its tires.

The Toyota rounded a corner, and the Sinclair Resort Hotel loomed into view. It hulked, monolithic, its imposing stone facade giving it solidity and presence, hardly bothered by the brutal storm surrounding it, just another one of thousands the building had weathered during its reign on its frigid mountaintop throne.

"Nice to see I'm expected." Up ahead, a single, dim light burned overtop of the resort's massive front doors. Lively pulled the 4Runner to a stop under a porte-cochere entrance which partially protected things from the elements. He killed the engine and stepped down from the SUV onto relatively snow-free cobblestones. A trio of low marble steps led up to the main doors. Dead leaves from Octobers past skittered along the base of these steps, dancing briefly with the swirling snow. Something colourful lay in the corner of the top step, slightly covered by windblown leaves.

Lively crouched down and brushed the detritus aside, then froze in place, saying, "Okay, then, this is an interesting start."

A colourful party hat, noisemaker and balloon rested in the corner of the steps, looking as if they'd just been laid out on a tabletop for an upcoming event here at the hotel. Recovering from the surprise, Lively stood, but left the party favours where he'd found them.

"Looks like the fun has begun."

With a click and a creak, one of the front doors popped open slightly, revealing a small sliver of darkened lobby beyond.

"And it looks like I'm invited."

CHAPTER FIVE

January 1st, 1982 1601 hours

A single chandelier illuminated one darkened corner of the grand ballroom. Looking over a small notebook, Inspector John Harder sat alone at a large, round table. A frown of concentration creased his brow as he attempted to decipher the chicken scrawl inside the notebook. It was his own, unfortunately. Pulling an always-ready HB pencil from behind his right ear, he scribbled away for a moment in the little black book.

In the distant lobby, a massive grandfather clock chimed five times, its sound muted by the heavy oak doors leading to the ballroom, both currently standing closed. Harder's stomach growled at the sound of the bell, and he realised he didn't remember the last time he'd eaten. He looked toward the tall plate-glass windows lining the far wall. Night had fallen, and the darkness outside caught him off-guard, so focused as he was on trying to make sense of it all. After almost twelve hours, he was no closer to understanding what had happened here than he was when he'd walked through the doors to this ballroom earlier this morning.

John's brow softened; his frown of concentration replaced with a look of sadness. Helen would be standing at the counter back at home right now, wrapping his dinner in numerous layers of tinfoil when she saw he wasn't coming home by six. With the day he'd had so far, he hadn't yet had a chance to let her know how long he was going to be. He would have to call her when he'd finished his current task and give her an update. His 'second brain' snarled, still contemplating the thought of the sweet and salty ham and cheesy scalloped potatoes just now being slid into the warm oven at home, begging to be eaten before it dried out.

Though he wasn't home with his wife for dinner, he was somewhat comforted by the thought that Helen knew in her heart that he would have been there for their meal by now, if it were at all possible. For the last twenty-five years of their marriage, he'd succeeded being there most nights, except when duty called. But still, it was on holidays he wanted to be with her most. Tonight, especially so, since it was also the anniversary of Danny's death.

Following in his father's footsteps, Danny, their only child, had joined the force as soon as he was out of college. One New Year's Eve while out on patrol, Danny had been in the process of checking an automobile for a suspected DUI. The driver had pulled over at a lookout located on a bluff high above the valley's ice-clogged river. While Danny stood next to the vehicle questioning the driver, another drunk had come along behind them and plowed into Danny and the DUI at full speed. The resulting fireball and explosion had killed the occupants of both vehicles and sent Danny hurtling into the river far below. His body had never been found. John and Helen were devastated. Since that day, the holidays had been something that held little joy for either of them.

John was preparing to listen to an interview of the ballroom's bartender, a man who had miraculously survived. After a few more minutes with his notebook, he removed his micro-cassette recorder from his briefcase and laid it on the tabletop. A cassette labelled 'J. O'Malley, 1st Interview' was already loaded, visible through the plastic viewing window on the recorder's front. John wanted to listen to what the bartender had to say in his own words, once again, while comparing it to his notebook.

This was the first of two separate interviews he'd done with the barman today. When interviewing in general, John liked to let a person ramble without too much prompting and just record them as they naturally recounted their experience, in order to see what spilt out. And in the case of bartender James O'Malley, it was more like a confessional.

Already suspiciously absent during the ballroom incident, it seemed James O'Malley might also be complicit in some of the events leading up to the disappearance, albeit in a small way. Harder pressed play, and a slight hiss could be heard from the recorder's single, small speaker as the tape began.

***

"This is a transcript of Bartender James O'Malley, conducted by Inspector John Harder of the Entwistle Detachment of the RCMP. Mr. O'Malley, could you please tell me, in your own words, about your experience here last night. Leading up to the event, was there anything different that happened that seemed out of the ordinary?"

"Well, the shift started out normally enough, I guess. As normal as anything can be around this place, I suppose. I tell you, in the five years I've been here, I've heard and seen things that seemed kinda weird, you know? As I said, this hotel is strange. There're these cold patches all over the resort. And it's usually never cold in the same spot twice, although there are a couple of places where it does happen pretty regularly. Must be that electric heat they use around here, kinda spotty, I guess.

Anyway, I've had a few occasions where I've come to work, everything seems fine, and then something just plain weird happens out of the blue. Like just after I first started working here and I needed to go somewhere in this creepy old place. Well, I ended up coming out in a different part of the hotel than I should have! I'm not a guy that gets easily lost, so I still don't understand that. One time, it was an entirely different floor. I swear, I feel like I'm going off my rocker with some of the bat-shit crazy stuff that happens around here. Oops, sorry for the expletive.

It was just before midnight last night, and I knew I was going to be here for another couple of hours, including cleanup time. They don't let us smoke on duty here just so you know. So, I thought since everyone is dancing and getting ready to kiss, this would be a great time to go out for a smoke; otherwise, I'd be lucky to get another chance for at least a couple of hours until my shift ended. I have to say, in light of everything that happened, now I'm glad that I hadn't quit smoking just yet, since one of my New Year's resolutions had been to give it up. Good thing I waited until after midnight, eh? Problem is, after this, I just don't know if I'm going to be able to quit again. At least, not for a while.

So, after I made sure nobody is approaching the bar, and everyone seems happy and dancy, I slipped out the fire exit in the corner of the room near the bar. I made sure to wedge a napkin in the door latch mechanism so I could pop back in and not get locked out. That had happened one time at a previous dance. I had a real hard time explaining to the front desk manager how I was supposed to be tending the bar in the ballroom, and yet there I was, sneaking back in the front door to get to my station. Doesn't look good, let me tell you.

Anyway, with the door almost shut behind me, I heard the countdown begin. I tell you, by the time I finally got my smoke lit in the wind I was almost getting ready to come in anyway since I was freezing my ass off out there. It must have been minus thirty at least last night.

Inside, a huge 'Happy New Year!' shout goes up and then the band begins to play Auld Lang Syne. There was clapping and shouting and laughter, for a second or so, then all of a sudden, the power goes out, and everything just stopped. Everything; all the sounds, all at once — like everyone just 'wasn't there' all of a sudden.

So, I snuffed out my smoke and headed back. I tell you, I had to grope my way along the wall to find the fire exit it was so dark outside, especially with the wind whipping the snow around like it was. The whole time, I kept listening for someone inside shouting about the power being out or needing a drink, but there was nothing at all.

When I got to the door, I stood there for a second, peeking through the gap. It was pitch black inside. And the cold! I swear the cold coming from inside that room seemed worse than outside, and it was pushing minus thirty like I said. But I just sort of stood there, despite the cold and the snow, not wanting to go in for a few seconds, and feeling very freaked out about everything. But it was strange, I also felt sort of electrified. Like I'd been touching one of those static generating balls they have at some of the science fairs. You know, makes your hair stand on end? Course that never works on me cause I don't have any!

Anyway, I'd had enough, and I pulled the door open all the way. Just then, the lights started to flicker back on.

And then I see the room was empty! I mean, what in the name of God happened to them? At first, I thought maybe everyone went to complain. But how could every last one of them leave the room in such a short time? One or two of them might go, I figured, but almost a hundred of them? It couldn't be. Someone would have stayed behind, I was sure. And yet the room was empty! Over on the other side of the ballroom, I see the kitchen manager and the new room service girl standing in one of the service doorways, staring back at me and looking as scared as I felt.

And the last thing I keep thinking of is the dance floor. You know? How the balloons and streamers that released at midnight weren't disturbed by anyone. Like they dropped into a room that was empty all along — as if there had never been anybody in there in the first place. But that wasn't possible because I was just serving them drinks! I mean, where the hell did they all go?"

"Thank you, Mr. O'Malley."

***

John stopped the tape and sat in thought for a moment. A little while after the first recording had been completed, the man had returned to tell him of another salient detail he'd neglected the first time through. Harder wanted to listen to that interview once more as well, since it concerned one of the strangest things in the ballroom, the ebony box.

It stood at the end of the bar, about one foot tall and black as midnight. The doors had at one time been sealed shut with black wax around all of its crevices. But most of it had been removed, with chunks of it lying on top of the bar. A heavy, ornate padlock ran through the two door handles on its front, however, keeping whatever secrets it still contained safely hidden away inside. It was strange, just like the rest of the box, its opening irregular, unlike the shape of any key John had ever seen. Intricate hieroglyphic designs were carved into the sides of its dark wood, with what looked to be pearl inlays running around the edges. Further markings were stamped into the black wax, one appearing to be the Star of David. After he'd cursorily examined the box this morning, it had been left undisturbed during the ensuing forensic sweep of the ballroom and hotel.

The wind kicked up outside and rattled at the windows. He looked out into the darkness, half-expecting to see the pale faces of the missing partygoers pressed against the glass, pleading to come in from the cold, or wherever they were now.

A sudden noise drew his attention toward the ballroom's huge mahogany bar, ending his contemplative glance out the window. In the silent room, the sound had seemed amplified. Only lasting for a moment, it sounded like dry leaves scraping across the ground in a gust of cold November wind. And it had come from the direction of the ebony box.

And then he heard it again — something was definitely moving about on the bar.

Harder rose quickly, cracking his kneecap against the table's underside. With a curse and a limp, he approached the lengthy bar. He reached for the Maglite on his belt, finding his pencil still in hand. He stuffed the short stub behind one ear absentmindedly and grabbed his light, turning it on as he did. It was much darker over here. When he'd seen the day growing long, he'd only turned on one set of lights this afternoon when he'd sat down at the table.

His beam flashed along the bar's highly polished surface, kicking up reflections and shadows on the snacks and beverages that covered it, making everything seem alive.

Several full drinks sat near bowls of peanuts, Hawkins Cheezies and other snacks scattered along the bar's length. Samples had been taken of everything here, including the entire smorgasbord and each drink and plate of food on the dining tables. John couldn't rule out that the missing persons may have been drugged, then kidnapped, even if there was no possible way they could have gone anywhere. He suspected a mouse had found some of this food irresistible. Sweeping the light back and forth rapidly, he couldn't see anything small, grey, or furry scuttling anywhere about.

John stood at the end of the bar studying the box. Somehow, it seemed different. Was it larger? In the shifting flashlight's beam, the delicate carvings on its sides seemed to coil and writhe with a life of their own.

The flashlight's beam quivered slightly in his hand, but it was not from fright, it was from cold. It felt as if the room's ambient temperature had dropped about thirty degrees over the last few seconds. His breath steamed from his nostrils as he reached out to touch the exterior of the box with one latex-gloved hand.

A sudden movement at the rear corner of the box made him pause and pull back slightly, his breath catching in his throat as he did.

In a blur of motion, something scurried up the side of the box. John jolted back, his heart trip hammering in his chest. He was a large man, not prone to sudden frights, but this was something different, something large, something terrifying.

The creature paused near the top for a moment, clinging on long, spiny legs. Multiple eyes regarded him with curiosity. Frozen in his light's beam, was a wolf spider so large, it looked as if it had just escaped the Paleozoic era and was now getting ready to catch something warm and juicy for its dinner. After a moment, the giant arachnid scuttled around to the back of the box out of sight.

Shuddering, Harder stood back from the bar, hesitating for a moment. He moved around the end and shone his light behind the mysterious box, the bar, and its shelves below, but he could see no further signs of the creature. The sweat from his forehead steamed into the preternaturally cold air, and he shivered once more. Where had it come from? Inside the box? But there was no way to open it that he could observe. He knew now he would have to examine it further.

On the floor, near the edge of the bar where the box sat, an obsidian gemstone glinted darkly in his light's beam. Had the stone come from the box just now? He didn't remember seeing it earlier. If he had, he would have bagged it as evidence. He picked up the gem, studying it briefly. His hand spasmed, and he dropped the stone to the ground. It had been freezing cold. A red mark now formed in the spot where it had briefly made contact with his skin, despite the rubber glove. He had used up his supply of evidence bags and pulled a linen handkerchief from his uniform jacket. He wrapped the gemstone inside with a sigh of relief and dropped the small bundle back in his pocket. He flexed his hand, still feeling the sting from the cold in his palm.

A tentative knock came from the service door across the room, and Harder jumped slightly. Corporal Jansen popped her head into the room. Hesitantly, the young woman said, "Inspector?"

Still vibrating internally from the shock of the oversized arachnid and the burn to his hand, John said, irritably, "Yes, what is it?"

With eyes as large as saucers, the corporal replied, "Inspector, there's something you need to see."

"Is it important, Corporal Jansen?" John could see the woman looked uncomfortable. He didn't know if it was because of what happened at the resort, or if perhaps she was still learning to be comfortable in her new rank within the RCMP. She was one of the first women in the RCMP to ever rise to the rank of corporal and had done so in just the last year.

"Yes, very important, Inspector." Jansen seemed to shrink back a bit as she spoke as if expecting Harder to bite.

Seeing the look on the girl's face, John softened his stern expression slightly, saying, "Sorry, it's been a long day."

"I can imagine, sir." She smiled slightly, her unease seeming to lessen a little, then concluded, "Please follow me, Inspector." With that, Corporal Jansen turned and left the room.

Though he came across as stern and unforgiving in his demeanour as well as his standards, Harder was quite pleased with the young corporal's performance within the RCMP so far. Until 1975, not a single member in an active front-line position as a peace officer had been a woman. When John had first learned that Jansen was being assigned to the Entwistle detachment, he was surprised and somewhat concerned. But Corporal Amanda Jansen proved her worth and abilities many times over in the ensuing months, and John was now proud to work alongside the young woman.

Jansen led John along the dim, concrete corridor to a small service elevator at the end. She pressed the call button, and after a brief moment, there was a ping, and the door to the elevator opened. Scowling into it before entering, John could only think of its interior as coffin-like. For some reason, the ornate fittings adorning the inside of the elevator reminded him of the brass handles and railings on the outside of a casket, something he'd become far too familiar with over the past few years, unfortunately.

"We need to go to the third floor," Jansen said, pressing a large, brass number three on the control panel. After the elevator doors slid shut, there was a squeal from one of the pulleys as the cage started to move upward, as if the ageing lift was protesting a man of John's 6' 3" stature being crammed inside its small space.

"The third floor? Why? What happened there?"

Amanda Jansen glanced up at Harder, her eyes seemingly wider than before, and said, "It's not what happened on the third floor, Inspector, it's what's still happening there."

CHAPTER SIX

December 23rd, 2021 2010 hours

Lively examined the intricate patterns adorning the massive, twin doors currently standing ajar before him. Intertwined leaves and vines were carved into their ancient, oaken panels. At first glance, it looked like a pattern befitting royalty, welcoming guests to the Sinclair. Looking more closely, Lively saw human faces filled with anguish and torment had been skillfully inserted amongst the entwined foliage. "Well, aren't you lovely," Lively said, shaking his head to the contrary. He wasn't surprised to see something like this, however, considering the history of this resort.

A self-made millionaire, Sinclair had the financial wherewithal to move huge sections of an ancestral castle in Scotland to the mountains of BC and incorporate them into his brand-new hotel. It would have cost a small fortune to have it hauled from such a distance, no doubt, but Sinclair could afford it.

Some of the work crew at the time had considered the resort to be cursed or haunted. But how, Lively wondered, could a new building have been haunted? He supposed it depended on several factors, including its location, building materials, as well as the person who designed and constructed it — they all could play a part. After several workplace accidents and disappearances, perhaps some of these things had left a psychic footprint behind? Possibly, but he couldn't know for sure at this point. He suspected that it may have more to do with Thomas Sinclair and whatever his ultimate intentions for this hotel had been.

One of Sinclair's first business ventures in Canada had been in the West Kootenays of British Columbia during the area's gold rush boom in the late

1890s. His saloons, casinos and brothels located around the town of Lawless and other gold mining communities had made him a very wealthy man. Back in the day, it truly seemed that everything Sinclair touched did indeed turn to gold.

As the boom faded, he'd diversified his holdings and constructed a luxury ski resort outside Lawless which had done exceedingly well for many decades. About ten years after the ski resort was completed, the Second World War broke out, providing more opportunities for Sinclair's enrichment. Like Coca-Cola, Bayer and Ford, the Sinclair corporation sold equipment, munitions, and supplies to both sides in the conflict — the Allies and the Axis powers. Of course, like the other corporations, Sinclair's involvement in supplying the latter didn't come to light until many years after the war. However, thanks to that extra bump in income, Thomas Sinclair had gone from millionaire to billionaire almost overnight.

After the war, he decided to try his hand at another resort, but this time near Entwistle, BC. With his newfound extreme wealth, the Sinclair Resort Hotel had been the result, a mega-resort, constructed to be the ultimate destination for the rich and famous on the West Coast of North America. And so it had remained — up until New Year's Eve 1981.

Lively peered into the beckoning darkness. After the door latch had popped open, he'd been on high alert for something else to happen, but it had remained quiet. He reached tentatively toward the large, brass doorknob, intending to push the door open a bit further.

He jerked his hand back suddenly, his fingertips numbed by intense cold. If he'd grasped the knob with any more solidity just now, he might have fused the skin of his fingers directly to the metal. He pulled on a pair of leather gloves that had been poking out from the oversized pockets of his bomber jacket. The temperature outside was well below freezing right now, but not so cold as to make the metal knob feel like it had been dipped in liquid-nitrogen.

Pushing the door open a little bit further with one now-gloved hand, he stuck his head into the gap and said, "Hello?"

He waited for a moment, then called out, "Anybody home?"

After several patient seconds of waiting and no response forthcoming, he took a half-step back, placed both hands in the middle of the large door and prepared to push it open. Without warning, the hinges squealed in protest and the heavy door swung inward, opening of its own volition as if an invisible doorman were bidding him welcome to the resort.

Standing in front of the now open door, Lively called out, "I'm Lively Deadmarsh. I was sent here to investigate what happened, and to hopefully help re-open this hotel."

No response appeared forthcoming and Lively felt a bit bolder, and he said, "Oh, I see. So now it's the silent treatment, huh?" With no immediate threat apparent, he stepped through into the hotel, then checked immediately behind the door, but no one hid there, as he suspected. He would have been surprised if someone had actually been here at the hotel. As far as he knew, no one had been inside this hotel since the police investigation had been put on hiatus almost forty years before.

"Is there anyone here?" Lively called out, his breath pluming from his mouth.

"Anyone here? Anyone here? Anyone here?" A series of shadow Livelys echoed his query from the building's cavernous depths, but only that and nothing more.

With a flash, Lively turned on an impressively bright mini-LED light he'd extracted from an inner pocket. He shone it along the wall behind the open door but didn't see what he was looking for. After a quick scan near the opposite door, he said, "Aha!" A series of clicks echoed throughout the vast lobby as he flipped a series of switches. Numerous lights flickered to life for the first time in decades. Unfortunately, they only illuminated the immediate foyer, and the Sinclair's furthest reaches still hid in deep shadow.

Lively's breath caught in his throat, feeling like Jonah inside the whale as he took in the grandeur of the massive hotel that had engulfed him. In a low voice, he said, "Spared no expense, apparently." He'd seen pictures of the lobby of the Sinclair from historical photos online, as well as crime scene photos, but they didn't do the actual interior of the building justice.

Three stories up, ornately painted ceilings vaulted across the massive lobby, disappearing into darkened recesses. Off to the left sat the front desk. A long and imposing piece of wood, it was set back underneath an airy mezzanine one floor above, with offices located at its back

Kitty-corner to the front doors, an elaborate cast iron and brass elevator sat with its doors open, patiently waiting for unseen guests. Directly opposite the entrance, a cobwebbed Christmas tree bereft of most of its needles wilted next to the closed doors of the Snowdrop Lounge. A faded banner ran overtop its doors, declaring in capital letters, 'SEASON'S GREETINGS!'

With a small smile, he said to the hotel, "Nice to see that despite everything else, you're keeping things seasonal around here."

Turning on the lights seemed to have helped somewhat with the cold, and his breath no longer steamed from his mouth. It was noticeably warmer in here now. The only sound was the slow drip of water. Looking down, Lively saw he was the cause of the precipitation. Snow from his fall near the gates had remained stuck around his jacket's collar and had just now begun to melt, dribbling down onto the floor. He brushed the remainder from his bomber jacket before the water soaked all the way through and stained the leather. The slush spattered onto the Italian marble floor at his feet, disturbing a thick layer of dust as it fell.

The Sinclair Hotel smelled old. Not just stuffy and unaired after forty years of closure, but ancient, like Tutankhamen's tomb must have smelled to Carter when he first opened it after millennia of isolation from the outside world.

"Let's hope there's not a curse in here, like ol' Tut's crib," Lively joked aloud, smiling slightly.

As if it had heard him, the hotel responded, and one of the bulbs in the decorative brass fixture over the front desk suddenly brightened, going supernova, then died and went dark.

"First it was power outages, and now it's power surges — what is it with this place and electricity?"

With unsure glances at the remaining lights in the fixtures, Lively moved behind the front desk, walking through a small breezeway at its side. A darkened office doorway stood open next to a plethora of pigeonholes where the keys and messages were kept. The hotel register lay on the desk, currently closed. Lively cleared some of the dust from the book's cover with a dramatic blow and opened it to the first page. After an explosive sneeze, he said, "Bless me," and began to leaf through the book.

The first page declared the register to be from December 1981. He let out a low whistle as he read through the list of celebrities and dignitaries that had filtered through the resort during the month. He flipped ahead until he arrived at the twenty-third of December — forty years ago this very night. He ran his index finger down the list of names and stopped short on the final entry, his breath hitching in his throat as he did. Filled in at the current time, but dated 1981, was a name he knew very well, written in a familiar hand, most likely using the pen chained to the mock inkwell on the desk in front of him. The darkened lightbulb above his head flickered and began brightening, returning to its former fully lit glory, spotlighting the name in the book for his viewing pleasure. In a low and unsteady voice, with all traces of mirth now gone, he read the name aloud, "Lively Deadmarsh."

CHAPTER SEVEN

January 1st, 1982 1705 hours

The elevator rose slowly toward the third floor, making John wonder if it was perhaps on its last legs. When the doors finally pinged open, he began to step out of the elevator.

Corporal Jansen put her arm out, saying, "This is only the second floor, sir." Across the large common area from the open elevator door, reflections of Harder and Jansen stared back at them from within a wall of floor-to-ceiling mirrors.

Harder stood confused. She was correct, they were indeed only on the second floor. However, the floor indicator overtop the doors inside showed a large number three brightly glowing, indicating they were supposed to be elsewhere.

"Things don't always go where they're supposed to around here," the young woman said, her voice hushed. She pressed the button for the third floor, and the elevator door slowly slid shut. With a small jolt, the car began to move upward.

After several long, silent seconds, with a slight jerk, the doors pinged open a second time. Despite the arrow inside indicating they were on the third floor, they found themselves all the way back down on the first floor. Harder frowned, this was making no sense. He'd felt the elevator move upward, and yet here they were, back where they started.

"There obviously must be a short in the button."

"It was working fine when I came down here to get you. Did you want to try the stairs?"

"Yes, hopefully, they're not out of order."

"You never know around here." Jansen stepped into the corridor once more.

Harder looked around the inside of the cramped elevator for a moment before exiting, then said, "But it is interesting, though."

"What's that?"

Stepping from the elevator back into the service corridor, Harder replied, "This is the same elevator that was in regular use last night, and none of the staff mentioned any issues or impairments of its function in their interview. One of them noted a chill inside of it, but that was the only thing."

"And yet it's acting up now. Perhaps it was affected by the power outage?" Jansen suggested.

"Perhaps..."

The service staircase to the upper floors was unremarkable. Stark concrete echoed their booted feet as they climbed the narrow stairs. On the third-floor landing, John paused, slightly out of breath and sweating lightly. "So — what exactly — is happening here?" he puffed questioningly.

Still appearing fresh and well-ventilated after the climb, the corporal replied, "I think it's best to just show you, sir."

Exiting the stairwell, they moved down another short, bare corridor that opened out into the hotel's guest area. The royal suite was at the end of a long hallway. Doors to dozens of suites were located along either side with branches leading to other wings of the hotel. A constable stood guard outside a door at the far end of the hall, his hat beneath one arm. The rest of his uniform looked like it fit him correctly about twenty pounds ago. Pudgy and balding, a single tuft of Tintin hair poked out from the top of his head. For some reason, constable Eric Eggelson looked very disturbed.

When he saw Harder and Jansen approaching his location, he stood a little straighter, patted down his tuft, and placed his hat back on top of his head.

"Inspector, Corporal," Eggelson said, nodding and addressing them as they arrived at the door. He sounded as unnerved as he looked, but his face showed some relief at not being alone up here on the third floor any longer.

"Constable Eggelson, what seems to be happening here?"

"I don't know sir. I haven't looked recently — haven't had the nerve," he admitted sheepishly.

"Move aside, please, constable." Harder approached the door, and Eggelson stepped off to one side. Facing the door, John grasped the doorknob. A penetrating cold numbed the palm of his right hand, freezing into the flesh. He jerked back with a sharp intake of breath.

"Sorry, Inspector, I should have given you these." Eggelson handed Harder a pair of industrial work gloves from his back pocket. "These make handling certain things around here a little easier," he concluded.

John looked at his right palm, the skin was red and looked like it might blister. He pulled the gloves onto his hands and turned the doorknob, but it wouldn't budge. "It's locked!"

"No sir, it isn't. I have the key right here." The constable pulled a silver key on a hefty golden fob from his pocket and handed it to Harder. "Try it for yourself!"

John jammed the key into the door lock and turned it, but discovered that the constable was indeed correct, it wasn't locked. The key moved freely. "What gives?"

Stuffing the key in his pocket, John grabbed the doorknob again, this time with both hands. Giving a mighty heave, he turned the handle with all of his might. The knob turned almost enough to disengage the lock and then it suddenly ripped back in the other direction, wrenched from Harder's grasp in the process, like it had been rotated by a pneumatic ram. Standing back in astonishment, John said, shocked, "Son of a bitch!" Over his shoulder, he said to Eggelson, "Is there anyone else up here with you?"

"No one, sir. I checked the suite myself about fifteen minutes ago when I first heard all the noises coming from the room up here."

"Noises?" Harder asked.

"Well, when I first came down this corridor doing a security sweep, it sounded like someone was having a life-or-death struggle inside there. But when I reconnoitred the room, it was empty." As Eggelson finished, a crash came from the other side of the door, and everyone jumped.

"What in God's name is going on here?" Harder asked.

Standing beside Harder, Corporal Jansen shuddered and said in a small voice, "I don't think God has anything to do with this."

John reached out to grasp the knob just as three rapid, heavy blows came from behind the closed door.

With a loud click, the knob turned, and the door suddenly popped open, just a fraction of an inch.

As one, all three police officers stepped back a pace. Nothing was visible, the dim light from the hallway doing little to illuminate anything more than a sliver of carpet inside the room.

Harder pulled his flashlight from his hip, along with his service revolver from its holster. He clicked on the light and clicked off the safety on the Smith and Wesson .38 Special. In an authoritative voice, he said, "This is Inspector John Harder of the RCMP, you are trespassing in a secured crime scene location. Come out with your hands up!"

Following John's cue, the junior officers drew their weapons as well, and each stood to one side of Harder.

John waited for a beat to see if there was any response.

The partially opened door remained unmoving, and the darkened room beyond was silent as a morgue.

Harder raised his size thirteen boot, its black, mirror-like finish gleaming in the brightly lit hallway. After a brief moment, he pistoned his leg outward. The heavy leather boot's rubber sole smashed into the door, slamming it back into the room. Something behind the door went crashing to the ground.

"That sounded expensive", John muttered under his breath, then ducked low and entered the room.

The two junior officers trailed Harder, each covering a different angle as they came through the open doorway behind him. Eggelson flipped the light switch next to the door, but nothing happened, and the room remained cloaked in darkness.

Spinning around three-hundred and sixty degrees with his light, John scanned the room for a perpetrator. Jansen and Eggelson swept the room at his flank, their own light beams cutting through the gloom on both sides simultaneously.

The room was empty.

Breathing hard, John's breath steamed like a locomotive, the temperature frigid inside the room. With a tilt of his head, Harder directed the corporal to move toward the partially closed door of the suite's half-bathroom. Jansen moved toward it slowly, gun at the ready.

John gestured to Eggelson to cover the closed bedroom door, giving him the hand sign to stand by at the same time, then he moved toward Jansen's location.

Harder booted the door, and with a crash, it pounded into the wall at its back, cracking the inlaid marble. The small, secondary bathroom was empty, with no place for anyone to hide.

A voice behind him called, "Inspector!" It was Constable Eggelson on the other side of the suite. The bedroom door had creaked open halfway while Harder and Jansen had been scoping out the bathroom.

Eggelson was on top of things, assessing the threat, and he moved toward the darkened bedroom doorway, gun at the ready. He suddenly looked energised by something he caught sight of in his light's beam through the opening, and shouted, "Freeze, police!" then lunged through the doorway.

"Eggelson! Stop!" Harder called.

With a resounding crash, the door to the bedroom immediately slammed shut behind Eggelson. Moving rapidly for a man of his size, Harder crossed the room with only a few long strides. Corporal Jansen was much more petite and had to move quickly to keep up with the inspector, like a small tug trailing an outgoing ocean liner on the coast.

Another forceful kick opened the bedroom door, and it tore partially from its frame, hanging drunkenly askew. As before, John moved in low, looking for feet or legs in his light's beam as he rapidly swept the darkened bedroom. Jansen slipped in directly behind him, instinctively covering the high side of things.

"Constable Eggelson! Where are you?" Harder called. They scanned the room with their high-intensity lights: more furniture and a massive bed, but no people. Somehow, the bedroom seemed even colder than the living area of the suite. John felt his nostrils freezing shut as he breathed. He turned around several times, repeatedly scanning the room as did the corporal. The heavy drapes were still closed, and Jansen pulled them open all at once, revealing a row of windows with blackness beyond. There were no other exits from the room, except for the ensuite bathroom.

With another thrust of his powerful leg, Harder rammed the bathroom door open with his foot, embedding its doorknob into the wall. "Police!" He shouted, flicking his light into the room, his adrenaline pumping. John hurried across the room and whisked the frosted glass shower stall door open. At the same time, Jansen covered a massive clawfoot tub in the other corner, but both locations proved empty.

Inspector John Harder stared around the room in disbelief, then looked toward Corporal Jansen. Her light green eyes returned his own look of utter astonishment, with her expression adding an element not seen in his own eyes, fear.

The Sinclair Resort Hotel's royal suite was completely empty. Constable Eric Eggelson had vanished without a trace.

CHAPTER EIGHT

December 23rd, 2021 2105 hours

Lively stood behind the front desk, back to the lobby, his courier bag slung over one shoulder. A brown American Tourister suitcase sat next to his legs like a faithful dog awaiting a scruff behind the ears. Before him, a panoply of passkeys sat in the pigeonholes of the cobwebbed wooden room-rack.

How many stories had occurred in each of those rooms, he wondered. Tens of thousands? Perhaps hundreds of thousands? And which of these suites would tell the most interesting tales? He'd investigated several hotels over the years that contained either a haunted room or a wandering spirit wailing about the place somewhere, but he'd never stayed the night in a place like the Sinclair, where so much had happened in such a relatively short period. After going over the police reports of the incident, and almost everything else concerning this hotel's darker secrets, he realised he was spoilt for choices in this 'incident prone' hotel.

Flummoxed, Lively studied the hotel's dusty rack. Three-hundred and forty-two available rooms, but which one to take for the night? "Well," he reasoned aloud, "either go big or go home, I suppose." He reached into the top pigeonhole and extracted a large silver key attached to a strangely shaped fob, which looked to be made of gold. After a huge sneeze from more disturbed dust, he said, "Bless me." Since there was no one else around to do so for him, he felt it important that he bless himself, particularly after a sneeze, and especially in this place. Not a superstitious man by nature, he still liked to cover all his bases, just in case. He turned around and faced the lobby, holding the key to the royal suite triumphantly in his right hand, and said, "The keys to the kingdom!" And then he sneezed again. With a sniff, he said, "Well, now I'm doubly blessed."

Extending the handle of his suitcase, Lively trailed it at his back as he crossed the large lobby toward the stairs. He paused before climbing to the royal suite and took a deep inhale, then coughed a little and wrinkled his nose in distaste. Thanks to his recent dose of dust. everything still smelled like an old library at the moment.

He was exhausted from his recent adventure on the high seas and ready for a good night's sleep. And although the last thing he felt like doing was exercising at this time of night, he was leery of taking the main elevator or any elevator in this hotel, for that matter. If he were the only person in the building and the lift decided to suffer a mechanical breakdown, or another power failure occurred, he'd be screwed. After a moment, he smiled slightly, thinking he would have to amend his thought in light of his destination and toss an adverb in front of it. He said aloud, "Actually, I'd be royally screwed."

Lively looked at the thick layer of dust on the carpeted stairs before starting his climb, and commented, "My, my, this looks like a job for Mr. Hoover, if ever there was."

Ka-bump... Ka-bump... Ka-bump. The suitcase's wheels slapped rhythmically against the steps as Lively's long legs conquered them one by one. Halfway to the second floor, the staircase opened out onto an expansive mezzanine that wrapped partway around both sides of the huge lobby. An enormous landscape of the resort took up most of one wall here. Behind a long-dead potted plant next to it, he found another series of light switches and flipped them up, banning the shadows that surrounded him. The painting depicted various events in each window: a dance in the grand ballroom and a swim in the pool, then chess in the games room, followed by lunch in the Snowdrop Lounge, all captured in minute detail.

"I'll have to play Where's Waldo with you tomorrow."

Much like the front door's extravagant engravings, he felt sure this portrait contained more than met the eye and could probably bear closer inspection. He wished Minerva were here since she loved this kind of thing. She had such different tastes from him, despite being his twin. Looking at this painting now, he knew without a shadow of a doubt that she would devour it with her eyes if she ever saw it. One of Minerva's 'things' was an attention to detail. She always loved Where's Waldo and easily solved them within seconds of looking at the drawings, most of the time. The longest she'd ever taken to find Waldo that Lively knew of was four seconds, and that was without her morning coffee.

After another short climb, he arrived on the second floor. An indoor terrace stretched out before him alongside a large, mirrored common area. On either side, an arcing staircase led up to the third floor. Choosing the right, Lively crossed the lengthy terrace and began the final leg of his ascent.

Ka-bump... Ka-bump... The suitcase followed him up the staircase as he climbed. But after a few more steps, the sound changed, becoming more resonant and bass-heavy.

Ka-BUMP... Ka-BUMP... This continued for several more steps, and then it became louder still.

KA-BUMP... KA-BUMP... Every time he climbed another step and his bag struck a stair riser, a mirroring retort would come from below, reverberating throughout the hotel. The sound grew louder and louder until the very building shook with every step he took, as if a giant had been stirred from its nap of ages and now clambered up from the bowels of the building, wanting to grind his bones for its bread.

Almost to the top, Lively stopped and looked back. Footprints, his own, stood out starkly on the dusty floor below. They meandered across the magnificent brocade carpeting, followed by a set of parallel lines on either side created by his suitcase's wheels. There were no other prints; however, that soon changed. He tugged the American Tourister up to the final step just below the top.

BOOM! At the bottom of the third-floor staircase, next to his dustprints, a massive invisible foot pounded onto the floor in front of the first riser, stirring up a mushroom cloud of dust.

Hair on the back of Lively's neck began to rise like the hackles on a cornered cat. The air felt electric around him as if he were surrounded by unseen high-voltage current. He took a final small breath, then pulled the suitcase all the way up to the third floor.

BOOM... BOOM... BOOM... Clouds of dust exploded up the stairs toward him as the entity accelerated its pace — no longer mirroring his steps, it now seemed very eager to meet him.

"You're on your own, little buddy," Lively said to his suitcase. He released his grasp on its handle and began an all-out sprint to safety. Slapping one sneaker-clad foot in front of the other, he raced down the hallway toward the salvation of the royal suite at its end. He grabbed for the room key in his jacket pocket as he moved, feeling its irregularly shaped fob almost immediately. All things considered, he wanted the key ready to insert into the lock when he arrived at the door and didn't want to waste any time fumbling for it in a panic. He risked a glance back over his shoulder as he ran.

Microcosmic dust storms exploded on the surface of the aged carpet as the entity pounded its invisible feet after him, moving fast and getting faster. Light globes lining both sides of the hall dimmed and then brightened again as it rushed by.

Hoping to pop it open, Lively slammed against the door with his six-foot-four frame, almost knocking himself to the ground from the force of his rebound. The door hadn't even quivered. But then again, why would it? This was the royal suite and would undoubtedly have reinforced doors to keep its occupants safe, not unlike a modern safe room, so he shouldn't have been surprised by the result of his driving blow.

He jammed the key into the lock and wrenched it to the right, disengaging the tumblers. With a yank, he extracted the key then slipped into the darkened room beyond. He leaned his full body weight against the door, slamming it hard. Within milliseconds, a filling-rattling crash came from the other side as the entity made contact with the heavy door, causing Lively to bounce off slightly from the impact. Fortunately, the reinforced concrete around the steel frame held. He reached his left hand behind his back and found the deadbolt, clicking it quickly closed.

Breathing raggedly from the unexpected exertion and adrenaline rush, Lively croaked, "Welcome to the Sinclair." He slapped the wall next to the door with his right hand, searching for the light switches for several long, dark seconds.

A trio of crystal chandeliers in the ceiling bathed the room in a sparkling rainbow of colours. "Let there be light." As the room came to full brightness, a final, jarring blow came from the other side of the entrance, followed by the sound of a heavy tread moving off down the corridor once more. It seemed his welcoming party had done its job and now had other duties to attend to elsewhere in the hotel.

Lively whistled softly, then coughed for a moment. He reached into his courier bag and pulled out a Salbutamol inhaler, taking a quick pull of its airway-clearing medicine. As he waited to regain a somewhat regular breathing rhythm, he took in the room around him in amazement. "Back in the day, this suite would have been the place to stay, if you were someone important. Well, tonight, I guess that would be me."

Throughout the vast, labyrinthine structure of the Sinclair, most amenities had been but a phone call away. But the royal suite was different from all the other suites; everything the hotel offered was available within fingers reach. Lively had read comments from several reputable sources that if the Sinclair couldn't provide whatever it was that you required immediately, somehow, they would make sure they found it ASAP, no matter what the request.

The room was as grandiose as he imagined it would be. Dust lay thick on every surface. The dated furniture and draperies smelled of age, like an elderly parent's closet full of dated clothes. There were a lot of antiques scattered around the room that Minerva would certainly appreciate, but he was not a fan, despite his retro leanings. On a sturdy table near the window sat a huge thirty-six-inch Sony Trinitron TV. Lively smiled, thankful that modern TVs were much more svelte than their bulky ancestors. He couldn't imagine carrying something that weighed more than he did up the flight of stairs to his condominium in the city. The seventy-five-inch, thirty-five-kilogram 4K TV hanging on his wall back home was awkward enough, thank you very much.

To aid in the relaxation experience, a fully stocked bar with lounge seating ran along one wall of the suite, backed by a massive ceiling-to-floor mirror. Dusty containers of nuts and bags of chips were surrounded by chocolate bars and other assorted candies on an ornate rack located next to the bar. Lively wandered over to look at them, his stomach starting to rumble. Quite a few of the items hadn't been available out in the real world for many years now. It was like a graveyard for discontinued snack foods; dusty brown plastic bags of Maple Buds nestled next to faded yellow and black-wrapped Neilsen Four Flavour bars, their labels peeling at the corners. On the shelf beneath, foil-encased King Dons reigned over several different varieties of Old Dutch potato chips.

Lively's stomach snarled at the sight of all the food. "Down, big fella." Despite his hunger, he wasn't going to risk eating decade-old chips or chocolate bars, unless he was starving and there was no other choice. Thankfully, he had come prepared and brought some high protein snacks to keep him filled up temporarily when hunger struck, but they were in his Tourister suitcase back in the middle of the hallway. He should have kept them in his messenger bag. — he loved how accurate his twenty-twenty hindsight was. If he were ravenous, there were some American MRE meals in the back of his 4Runner, but he didn't feel like getting them tonight, all things considered. Still, he would need to do something about the food situation soon and at least get a snack from his suitcase before bedding down for the night.

The furnishings in the royal suite were eclectic, to say the least. Different periods clashed with each other in a war of the ages. Near the bedroom door, King Louis XIV armchairs flanked Elizabethan end tables. In the far corner, an imposing Chippindale credenza towered over a Napoleonic knick-knack cabinet currently sitting empty.

There was damage to the bathroom and bedroom doors, looking like someone had tried to break them down with their foot, judging by the big black boot prints on them. "Must have been quite the evening," Lively said in a low voice.

Lively moved into the bedroom. A circular bed that looked about the size of Vancouver Island sat on a raised platform in the middle of the room. At his back, the wall was covered with yet another floor to ceiling mirror. Moving to the ensuite bathroom revealed a full, frosted glass shower next to a toilet and an ornate bidet. Across the black and white tiled floor, a colossal clawfoot soaker tub with feet like eagle talons sat on yet another platform. To Lively, it looked more than ready to scrabble down from its perch and go on the hunt for fresh prey to drown in its voluminous recesses. Whatever else you had to say about this place, he mused, the Sinclair Resort Hotel's high-end suites didn't skimp on raised platforms on which to display their massive beds and horrifically designed bathtubs.

Despite having emptied his bladder at the gate, it started squawking again at the sight of the toilet, creating a new sense of urgency. The three cans of root beer he'd drunk, almost in a row, were not finished with him yet it seemed. Before he had any accidents, Lively decided to use the facilities while he was in the appropriate room. He left the door open at his back as he urinated. Shortly, a shudder went through his body, and he sighed in relief as things trailed off to a thin dribble. "Ah, the pause that refreshes."

The bathroom door behind him suddenly pounded shut, closing so forcefully that it cracked the tile accents around the doorframe's edges.

Lively jumped as if electrified, spraying some of his remaining Barq's wildly across the toilet seat and floor next to it. He quickly got things back under control, zipped and turned at the same time, expecting someone or something to be standing behind him, but there was no one there.

He tried the doorknob and found it turned freely. After a bit of a pull to dislodge the door from the frame, he peeked out into the suite.

The room stood empty.

Looking as startled on the outside as he felt on the inside, another Lively Deadmarsh peered back at him from the mirrored wall opposite. "Caught you by surprise too, eh, buddy?" he inquired of his reflection, laughing slightly, and shaking his head. The Lively across the way shook his head in commiseration, matching his movements and laughing slightly as well.

Moving through the doorway from the bathroom into the suite, across the room, his doppelganger did so as well. They both approached the king-sized bed in the centre of the room. In both of their universes, something had changed in the room.

The enormous circular bed had a new occupant, the American Tourister suitcase.

A series of disturbances in the thick layer of dust on the carpet around the bed were evident. "Looks like my heavy-footed friend is playing bellhop and making luggage drops now." He looked up toward his mirror-mate a final time, saying, "I guess that's part of the full-service package they provide around here." His reflection looked back at him, grinning widely, and enjoying the joke.

Lively froze.

There was one small problem. When he'd made his lame joke just now, he hadn't smiled.

But his reflection had.

And it still was.

CHAPTER NINE

December 24th, 2021 0725 hours

Strains of Bach's Brandenburg Concerto drifted from the BMW's powerful sound system as Minerva Deadmarsh wove the Alpina XB7 through the winding highway's curves. Although she exceeded the posted speed limit on occasion (okay, on most occasions), she didn't consider it speeding. Speeding implied driving with reckless abandon, but she never did so — she only drove with control and finesse.

Her three-hour nap last night just wasn't cutting it. She sipped the steeped tea she'd picked up at the Tim Hortons in Entwistle, glad to have something hot to keep her awake. Fortunately, she hadn't had any issues so far, and the XB7 had swept her through the deep snow in the narrow lane that led up to the Sinclair Resort with no difficulty whatsoever. Then again, for what the SUV cost, she hoped there wouldn't be an issue.

After purchasing the BMW, when she'd first told Lively the model's name, he'd joked with her that the XB stood for 'Xtra Bucks', of which a person needed a profusion in order to own one. There weren't many things that Minerva spent her money on in life, but a nice ride was one of them. When her brother bought vehicles, he only wanted something reliable and serviceable. She, on the other hand, wanted something safe and stylish. The fact that this vehicle cost almost as much as her small condo in Yaletown was beside the point.

Her flight had been delayed several hours by the storm, and she'd arrived in Vancouver much later than she'd wanted last night. After her plane finally landed, she'd dropped by her apartment and picked up a few things she might need, along with a few hours of sleep. The weather office had predicted the storm would break overnight and she wasn't the sort of person to risk life and limb to get somewhere a couple of hours earlier, fighting against inclement weather, unlike her more thrill-seeking brother.

But it wasn't that she didn't like thrilling things as well. She was an amateur rock-climber in addition to her other talents, so she knew what adrenaline was when she felt it. She'd picked up the hobby from one of her roommates in college, Christine Moon. Minerva had always been a person who liked to know the risks when she did something. That's what appealed to her about rock climbing — you're continually assessing the rockface ahead as you plan your ascent, looking for the safest and fastest route, most of the time. Manageable risk, she figured, was where it's at.

Already the kind of person to be up before the dawn, today Minerva had risen extra early. This was one of the shortest days of the year. It had been pitch-black outside when she'd left the city, the sun not yet ready to peek over the horizon for several more hours. Unfortunately, this early day would cause her to miss out on her morning yoga practice. But her downward dog would have its day again sometime soon, of that she was sure. It was all worth it, though, just to be able to sneak up on her unsuspecting brother and surprise him.

The resort's entrance appeared around a final bend in the winding road, and Minerva slowed her BMW to a crawl. One of the gates stood open and she could see faint tracks in the snow from another vehicle going through many hours earlier. The snow lay thick in the lane, but she felt confident the Alpina would do its job and get her up to the hotel safely.

At over two hundred acres, the resort's property was enormous. The massive hotel suddenly came into view and she gasped. It sat in the centre of a large clearing, flanked by old-growth forest on either side. Imposing and cold, its rough stone exterior stood exposed and naked to the world. It seemed made of nothing but sharp angles, each one jutting out starkly against the brilliant blue of this post-blizzard day. Currently bathed in dazzling golden light that flooded over a serrated series of mountain peaks in the east, the building's castle-based origins were more than evident. On the ramparts that ran along its top, she expected to see vats of boiling oil ready to pour over any barbarian hordes that might happen to wander by. Wherever there were windows along the ground level, they were boarded over with exceedingly sturdy looking lumber, presumably to keep vandals or looters out of the place. A huge snowdrift ran up the side of the building at the far corner, stopping near the base of a second-story window. Minerva smiled, thinking it looked like an excellent room to check into with your bag under one arm and a Crazy Carpet tucked under the other.

A green Toyota 4Runner sporting a yellow bumper sticker on its back hatch sat parked beneath the hotel's covered entrance. Minerva smirked slightly as she got close enough to read the sage words on the sticker, 'Sometimes, I struggle with my personal demons, other times we just snuggle'. Her big brother had apparently made it up here safely last night after all. As to what happened to him since he got inside, she was about to discover.

Surprising Lively was one of the things she enjoyed doing in life, but it could be quite challenging. Despite her best attempts to fool him, he almost always seemed to know what she was up to. But not today. She figured this time really would be a surprise since Lively had no idea she was now part of this investigation.

After her brother had signed on, she had been contacted about participating in the investigation as well. Minerva assumed he had come on board under similar contractual circumstances to hers. She'd been asked to sign a nondisclosure agreement not to share her participation in this investigation or share the outcome publicly. Along with the NDA had been an appropriately dumbfounding amount of money offered for her acceptance, and a disclaimer of equally steep penalties if she were ever found in breach of the agreement.

Minerva had done her fair share of research regarding the Sinclair incident over the years, just like Lively. She could understand the trepidation on the part of the holding company regarding safety and liability issues before their tentative reopening.

Back in 1985, after several years of legal wrangling, the lawsuit had been settled between the relatives of the missing people and the Sinclair Development Corporation. The company had been found liable for negligence, and the victim's families had received almost two-million dollars each. A tidy sum to be sure back then, these days it would have been closer to six million per person. After the settlement and all of the court costs were tallied up, most of the Sinclair Corporation's capital had been wiped out, and bankruptcy had ensued.

With liability payouts these days usually in the billions, she could understand the desire for the resort's holding company to keep things as safe as possible and as quiet as possible. If they were to reopen, they didn't want to have any repeats of the past and wanted to know that the building was 'safe'. Safe was a relative term, Minerva realised when it came to paranormal events in a building like the Sinclair. Until she, Lively, and whoever else may be involved in the investigation could determine what might have caused the incident, they could offer no assurances one way or the other that it wouldn't happen again in the future.

Much like her reason for taking this offer, it was also the reason she had been in Ireland for the last week — to verify the paranormal status of a heritage building. It had been something she'd been doing more and more of lately, utilising her gift to help out where she could. Some clients wanted to verify they had a supernatural addition to their property, first, before buying it, while others wanted to know what they needed to do to get rid of it. She hadn't been making a career out of things like this in the same way Lively seemed to be doing since he resigned from CSIS. That being said, she didn't object to assisting someone if they approached her, and they wanted to pay her as well. And that is what happened here. For her personally, this one contract would set her up almost for life, paying her condo fees and keeping her in BMW XB7s for many years to come.

The reason for her visit to the Emerald Isle had been to help out a good friend of hers from London who was looking to purchase an ancient public house and inn. This pub was also pitched as being very haunted. Her friend, Angus McGregor, wanted someone with her abilities to verify the claim and stay there for a few nights, and hopefully make a recommendation. But after what happened in the rooms above the pub on the first night of her stay, Minerva had been more than ready to whole-heartedly endorse the place well before her flight back to Canada had been ready to depart.

The Dublin job had been exciting and dangerous, especially for someone with her more sensitive abilities. When she'd been there, she'd figured she had never before been in a more haunted building. That was until now, with her upcoming visit to the Sinclair. What exactly had happened in that resort's grand ballroom on New Year's Eve 1981? No one knew, and they could only speculate. The only thing everyone agreed upon was that it was one of the most intriguing and shocking paranormal events ever recorded. And now, Minerva was going to attempt a reading there, amongst other things, to help make sense of this midnight of madness known as the Sinclair Incident.

She placed her Alpina in park behind the 4Runner and killed the engine. The SUV was relatively high off the ground, sporting twenty-three-inch wheels, but Minerva had no trouble climbing down out of it, thanks to her long, leather boot-clad legs. Though she was Lively's twin, they were not identical. However, one of the things they did share in their dizygotic relationship was their height genetics. Although not as tall as Lively's six-foot-four, at five feet, eleven inches tall, Minerva towered over most men when wearing even her most modest, three-inch heeled boots. A strikingly beautiful woman with auburn hair and piercing hazel eyes, she was as gorgeous as her mother, or so she was told. Selene Deadmarsh had died giving birth to her twins, never revealing to anyone who their father was before her passing. Minerva and Lively had been raised by their maternal grandparents in Vancouver, and had grown up always wondering of their heritage, but never knowing anything for sure.

Old photos and motion pictures were now the only way for them to remember the mother they'd never met. From what Minerva had seen, Selene Deadmarsh had been as talented as she was lovely. A model by trade, her mother had also been an up-and-coming actress in the growing 'Hollywood North' entertainment industry. Before her untimely passing, Selene had made several films and guest-starred on quite a few TV shows, finally getting noticed more and more by actual Hollywood studios down south. Following in her mother's footsteps, Minerva had done some modelling herself and been paid quite well for it when she was younger, but unlike her mother, acting never held any appeal for her.

Minerva closed the door of the SUV and stood for a moment, stretching, and breathing deeply. She hadn't been out of the XB7 since she'd left the city and still felt electrified by the drive. Clean mountain air filled her lungs, scouring them of the pollution from living in the city. The air was stingingly cold up here since the storm had cleared. According to the Alpina's external temperature sensor, it was currently sitting at minus twenty-nine Celsius, and that was without the bitter wind that currently buffeted Minerva's faux fur coat. She shivered, wanting to get inside the hotel as quickly as she could.

Something caught her attention near the top corner of the stairs leading to the front doors. A deflated, golden-coloured balloon with an uncanny resemblance to shrivelled skin partially covered a striped noisemaker and party hat sitting next to it. She shook her head. "Lively's already gone and gotten this party started without me. How typical."

The front doors to the resort were hideous. As soon as Minerva saw them, she couldn't unsee the grotesquely carved faces that had immediately leapt out to her observant eye. She shook her head, supposing it was somebody's idea of fine art. Fortunately, one of the doors was unlocked, and she didn't have to look at them long. The knob turned freely, and she pushed one of the heavy doors inward, following it through into the hotel.

Minerva closed the door firmly to keep the cold out, then turned back toward the cavernous lobby. Her breath caught in her throat and her eyes seemed unable to blink. The opulence on display was mind-numbing. She couldn't remember the last time she'd seen so much stone, marble, and brass together in one place. Her lungs suddenly remembered to breathe, and she let out a small gasp, finally blinking her eyes several times as well.

The chandeliers overhead shone bright as day, flooding the corners, and banning any shadows in the vast expanse of the lobby. But something felt 'off' in here. Perhaps it was because it was so bright, overly so, almost. But no, she shook her head, that wasn't it. And then it dawned on her. Somehow, it was larger on the inside of this building than it appeared on the outside, and it was already huge to start with.

What she thought she was seeing didn't seem possible. It reminded her of one of the shows that Lively liked to watch with the time-travelling Doctor and his portable man-cave that was bigger on the inside than it looked on the outside. The hotel lobby seemed like that right now, almost too much so, in fact.

More fresh air seemed like a great idea right now. She needed to have a moment to reset, then try this again.

Minerva turned and felt her reality slip. The doors were a hundred feet behind her and stretching further into the distance by the second. She spun back toward the lobby. An impossible amount of shining marble floor lay between her and the front desk. The elevator across from it looked suddenly minuscule from an increasing gap, and the stairs appeared as remote as the surface of the moon.

She closed her eyes and began to count to ten. When she opened them, she hoped to see a lobby of regular proportions surrounding her instead of this Whovian Tardis that now stretched out to infinity in every direction.

CHAPTER TEN

"Hail Mary, full of Grace,
the Lord is with thee.
Blessed art thou among women."

January 1st, 1982 2355 hours

Since his first day on the force, John Harder had been a pragmatic and logical man, prone to believing what he saw with his own two eyes, rather than relying on hearsay or second-hand information. But that being said, he also found there was much more to the world that remained unseen than just what he saw with those same eyes. What he'd observed so far since arriving this morning at the Sinclair had shaken him to his very core.

John had been brought up in a strict Catholic household that had contained minimal joy. His mother had been a devout Christian with all the trimmings, including crucifixes over the beds, figurines of Mother Mary holding Baby Jesus in the living room and a painting of the Last Supper on the dining room wall. John wasn't as convinced of God's divine power as much as his mother had been, but he still took some comfort in the concept.

However, something that made him feel downright uncomfortable was the disappearance of Constable Eric Eggelson. This hotel had felt bad when he'd walked through the front doors earlier this morning, about a half a lifetime ago, and it felt even worse now.

Standing in the centre of the ballroom, with all of the lights on this time, John slowly turned, surveying the room. Beyond the tall windows, swirling snow travelling on icy wind rattled at the emergency doors and tapped at the glass as if the missing partygoers were just outside, freezing to death and desperate to get back to the light and warmth. He shuddered.

Earlier this morning, RCMP members had combed the forest surrounding the resort for the missing persons. Others had questioned the remaining patrons that hadn't been in the ballroom. Several guests and staff had been referred to Harder for follow up, once it was established that they had information which might be of value. After the remaining guests had been thoroughly vetted, he'd released them by noonhour, and they had been glad to go. The support staff had been interviewed next, with the last of them being released by dinner time.

One of the most important people they had been searching for had been Thomas Sinclair's surviving son, Edward. He had been scheduled to appear at the party and participate in some of the celebrations. Unfortunately, he, too, was missing in action. As a result of this, the resort's senior management had quite understandably decided to shut things down temporarily to afford the police time for their investigation.

All staff and customers had been placed under a strict gag order in regard to speaking about what had occurred at the hotel until the RCMP were ready to make an announcement — and that had to be soon. John knew when this got out to the media, all hell would break loose up here. A local reporter, Will Weston, had shown up sniffing about, just around the time the last of the staff had been released. After some negotiation with Weston, John had managed to have the man hold his press release for twenty-four hours, and in exchange, John said he would give him an exclusive interview.

For now, it was quiet both inside and out. Weston had kept his word, and no members of the media were anywhere in the vicinity. Silence was John's only companion, and he was alone inside the hotel. Only one other RCMP member was still on the property. Corporal Amanda Jansen was currently stationed outside the front door, sitting in a heated police cruiser. When he was done for the day, which looked to be any minute, he would let Jansen know that outside was where he wanted her to stay. He didn't want anyone inside this hotel tonight if he could help it, all things considered.

John had seen how shaken the corporal had been by Eggelson's disappearance this afternoon, and after another search of the hotel for the missing constable, he'd wanted to send her home for some rest. But instead, she'd immediately volunteered to be here on guard duty for the night. John had given her a key to a clean suite that the management had provided to them in the event someone needed rest. About an hour ago, she had awoken and informed him that she would be outside in the cruiser. He suspected she was feeling guilt, which he shared, over Eggelson's disappearance. The young woman was dedicated, despite her fears of this place. John was quite impressed with her fortitude and knew she would go far in the force.

He stood at the windows looking out into the bitter January evening. Smooth, unblemished snow blanketed the ground outside the windows and exits. If all the people had run out of the room, or even tried to in those fifteen seconds, the snow would have been a trampled mess outside the windows as well as the emergency exits. But there didn't appear to be a snowflake out of place near any of them. And that hadn't changed since the last time he'd looked this morning. In the window's reflection, John saw a somewhat despondent looking RCMP inspector frowning back at him.

The insanity that had started in the ballroom at the stroke of midnight last night had never apparently ended. With the unexplained pounding in the royal suite followed by the disappearance of Constable Eggelson from a room with no visible exits, things just kept getting weirder and weirder around here.

When he'd first arrived this morning, John had had some of the constables go knocking on the suite's doors, verifying which rooms, if any, contained guests from the ballroom. Apart from the seventy rooms booked by the ball's attendees and musicians, the hotel had been almost empty. There had only been about a dozen other guests staying here, most who had come to relax at the resort after Christmas. Some of them had celebrated the new year in their suite, while others had partied in the Snowdrop Lounge. And some had elected to have more privacy and had chosen to remain in their suite. Vivian Aubergine was one of those people, staying on the third floor of the hotel, next to the royal suite. The event which she experienced had seemed quite pertinent to the case, as she'd reported something exceedingly strange happening when midnight struck.

Needing to hear her recount her tale once more, John extracted his microcassette recorder from his pocket then sorted through the cassettes in his briefcase to find her recording.

In her late fifties, Aubergine was an attractive woman with spiked, short hair dyed jet-black to hide time's advances. Smartly and expensively dressed, she was also very well-spoken, with just a hint of a French accent. Unlike some of his other interviewees, she had been somewhat reluctant to talk, and he had to prompt her a bit more than the others, who had pretty much rambled on of their own volition the entire time.

Blowing into the microphone, John heard himself say, "Interview with Vivian Aubergine, guest of the hotel, staying in suite number three-thirty-one, directly adjacent to the royal suite."

***

"The reason I decided to spend the holidays up at this lovely hotel, instead of on the East Coast like I usually do, is because I didn't feel strong enough, emotionally, to go to any parties alone this year. Sadly, this is my first New Year's since Phillip passed."

"I'm so sorry. How long were you and your husband together?"

"My Husband? Who said anything about a husband? Phillip was my Pomeranian!"

"Oh, I'm so sorry. Well, still, that's unfortunate. Please, I'm sure it's hard, but if you could summarise for me what happened to you in your suite at midnight last night?"

"Thank you, Inspector. Well, first of all, in answer to your question, Phillip and I were together for fifteen years and I missed him terribly. In any event, I'd wanted to have a low-key evening, and had just received my room service at half-past the hour, just like I'd requested. I must say, that is one of the pluses of this hotel. They are always so punctual with their food delivery, amongst other things."

"You received it at 11:30?"

"Yes, Inspector, that's usually when half-past occurs. Anyway, it was delivered by an enchanting young Spanish girl, I can't recall her name exactly, Imelda, I think perhaps?"

"Esmeralda?"

"Why yes, I think that was it! Lovely dark-haired little thing! Thank you, Inspector. So, anyway, I decided to get ready for bed before partaking in my midnight repast, and by the time I was finished, it was just a couple of minutes before the ball was ready to drop. I like to tune into the revelry in Times Square each year if I am not there to take part. So, the countdown started, and I had just popped my champagne open. I quickly poured a glass and got it raised in the air just in time to toast in the new year. When the ball hit bottom, and everyone shouted, 'Happy New Year', I was about to take my first sip, then the power went out. And that's when I heard this noise from the royal suite next door."

"What kind of noise?"

"A kind of popping sound. At first, I thought it sounded like someone next door popping open a Methuselah."

"I'm sorry? A Methuselah?"

"Yes, a six-litre bottle of champagne. I often have them when I have a larger party of guests. They make a very distinctive noise when they're opened."

"Thank you for the clarification, Ms. Aubergine."

"Yes, of course. But I wanted to add that this noise was, while being close to the sound of a Methuselah, it wasn't quite the same. This was much deeper than how that cork pops, so I dismissed the idea of that being the noise almost right away. I'm not sure if you have noticed, but there are no emergency lights in the suites, only in the halls, which is something that should be addressed, in my opinion. Anyway, it was pitch black in the room, and I didn't know how long the power would be out. Since I didn't want to stumble over something in the dark in an unfamiliar room, I just decided to wait it out and stay where I was for a little while. And that's when I heard it and almost saw it."

"Heard what? Saw what?"

"Over at the entrance to my suite, near the crack at the bottom of the door, I could see the faint light from the emergency lights out in the hallway..."

"Go on, please."

"Well, the door to the royal suite opened with such a bang and slammed against the wall, I didn't know what to think. And then... And then 'something' came out of that room. It made hardly any noise, but I could hear the floor creaking as it moved along, so it must have been quite heavy. And I know that it paused in front of my door."

"How do you know?"

"All of the light under the crack at the bottom disappeared."

"Disappeared? All of it? You mean this thing blocked out the light because of its size?"

"No, I mean it was like it took all of the light with it as it moved. After it passed, the emergency lights outside in the hall slowly flickered back on. That's not something that they would have done if they had only been blocked by something standing there."

"What did it do then?"

"I heard it thump off down the corridor, moving away, faster and faster like it was running late for a very important date. I have to tell you, whatever it was, I am glad I wasn't the target of its attention."

***

John flipped the notebook closed and looked out the windows. In the reflection, he could see the box sitting on the end of the bar where he'd left it since he'd had his experience in the royal suite. He sighed and looked at his watch, surprised to see it was almost midnight. He wanted to examine that infernal box again, but not tonight. He would have to do so tomorrow. Eighteen hours had elapsed, and he was mentally and physically exhausted.

His mind was awhirl as he looked around the huge ballroom. Just two dozen hours ago, it would have been filled with happy revellers, celebrating their successes in the old year, and looking forward to more of them in the new. And then midnight struck... And then what?

Was that thing that Aubergine reported moving past her suite's door related to the event that transpired down here in the ballroom? And if so, did it somehow facilitate or participate in the mass disappearance when it got down here? Could it be connected with Eggelson's disappearance as well, he wondered. John shook his head in confusion.

With muted chimes beginning to ring, the grandfather clock in the lobby proclaimed it to be the witching hour. After four chimes of the clock, the lights dimmed to a dull yellow colour, but didn't extinguish completely.

Something suddenly caught the corner of Harder's eye, moving around outside the window in the swirling, blowing snow. He squinted, looking closer and realised it wasn't something moving outside in the dark of night, it was something moving around inside behind him.

He twirled and scanned the room, eyes wide. There was nothing he could see out of the ordinary anywhere, but it wasn't as easy to see into the far corners of the room now with the lights remaining dim from the power drain.

John turned back to the window, gazing intently into the room's reflection. The mahogany bar was clearly visible at his back. But it wasn't the bar he was looking at in stunned silence. He spun and looked about the room again. There was clearly no one near the bar, or anywhere else that he could see.

Returning his gaze to the window, John Harder began reciting the Hail Mary, and he crossed himself.

Reflected behind him, as if seen through a sheet of gauze, a roomful of beautiful people twirled and swayed to the sounds of an unheard orchestra, celebrating the beginning of the first day of a new year, a day which for them, appeared to have no end.

CHAPTER ELEVEN

December 24th, 2021 0735 hours

A sliver of daylight beamed through the heavy drapes off to one side of the room. Lively cracked one eye open and looked about for a moment. He closed that eye and opened his other, lifting his arm to his face to see his wristwatch. He felt disoriented, and the room seemed like it was spinning around him. Both eyes now closed, he draped his right forearm across his eyes for a moment.

Apparently, he'd slept for almost nine hours. But he didn't remember going to sleep. In fact, the last thing he remembered was seeing himself grinning in the mirror like a looney-tune. He was currently lying underneath the covers of the massive circular bed. On his recent optical reconnoitre, he'd spied his clothes folded neatly, sitting on one arm of a wingback chair across the room. Feeling around beneath the covers for a moment, he discovered that apparently included his underwear. Currently sitting closed, his suitcase was now on a lowboy dresser next to the chair. The bed's dusty duvet cover had been neatly folded back and lay draped across his feet. And yet, he had no recollection of folding the cover down or even getting undressed for that matter. The sheets under which he lay, though clean looking, were slightly yellow and smelled heavy with the must of age.

However, he wasn't really surprised he'd fallen asleep so easily. His cruise ship shenanigans must have taken their toll on his energy levels. For some reason this morning, he felt much more lethargic than he usually did after such an experience. Usually, by the next day, he felt his regular self, but strangely, that was not the case today, and he still felt drained.

Lively's stomach rumbled in an alarmingly aggressive manner, and he realised he hadn't had anything to eat, either. With his metabolism, he'd be burning away what little body fat he had fairly quickly. He'd been basically fasting since touching down in Vancouver harbour yesterday afternoon. Though he'd taken advantage of fasting's benefits when he'd been on a desk job for a few months in the past, he didn't need to lose too much weight right now, not so soon after such a taxing time on the cruise ship. Food would be his first order of priority once he became vertically oriented once more.

Still, he wished he remembered how he got to bed. He was not prone to lapses in his memory unless copious amounts of alcohol were involved, which was a rare thing. But he hadn't imbibed in anything more potent than Barq's Root Beer last night, and he doubted that three cans would do it. He put his vision of himself grinning in the mirror down to a hallucination brought on by exhaustion. And although he now knew powerful entities were running around the halls here, he felt fairly certain that there weren't parallel dimensions existing in the mirrors or anything like that, or were there?

Lively tried to sit up, but the carousel on which the bed seemed to be currently located started to revolve again, and he lay back down. With his forearm now draped across both eyes, he said aloud, "Man, I don't even need to have something to drink to feel hungover around this place. Maybe I need to switch to water. I think Barq's has too much bite."

A voice across the room said, "Water is where it's at, Big Brother."

Lively jerked his arm away from his eyes and looked up with surprise to see his sister leaning in the doorway to the bedroom, watching him.

"Minerva! What are you doing here? And how did you know I was up here?" Despite feeling like he was on a Tilt-A-Whirl, Lively pushed himself all the way upright as his sister walked into the room. He propped several pillows up at his back, and the bedsheets fell onto his lap.

"Well, first of all, I was contacted and made an offer I couldn't refuse, just like you, I'd imagine." Minerva entered the room, flipping the light switches on as she came through the doorway, causing Lively to shield his eyes from the glare.

"This is true, but I would have done it for free. I've never wanted to solve anything more in my life than what happened here," Lively said, adjusting the bedsheets around him.

"Oh, I know that, Big Brother. And in answer to your second question, I looked in the key rack and the only key missing was the key to this suite, so I made like Sherlock Holmes, deduced my deductions, and here you are!" She gave him a brief smile and unwrapped her shoulder-length auburn hair from a multicoloured silk scarf that strained to contain its lush volume. Unslinging a small, purple backpack purse from her shoulder, she stuffed the scarf inside, then sat on the edge of the round bed near Lively, bouncing gently on the mattress for a moment as if to test it. She looked around the enormous bedroom and said, "I see you found yourself some modest accommodations." She looked to the bedroom door, hanging slightly askew in its frame, a black boot print in its centre. "Did I miss all the fun here last night?"

"Is that what it was?" Lively smiled somewhat cryptically and then said, "It was like that when I got here, honest." He reached over and gave his sister a large hug saying, "It's great to see you, Minerva. I'm really glad you could be here."

"Not a problem, Big Brother." She hugged him back. "I'm almost as curious about this place as you, being inundated as I was with facts and figures about it when we were growing up, thanks to you!"

"You're right. It's my Holy Grail — something I've wanted to investigate my entire life, and now I'm finally getting the chance! It's like I'm at the Stanley Cup, sitting next to Wayne Gretzky, Gordie Howe and Tim Horton, and drinking a Moosehead beer!"

"That does sound pretty exciting." Minerva stood and walked to the window. "You do realise Gordie Howe and Tim Horton are dead, right?"

"I know, but I don't hold that against them." Finally standing upright, Lively wrapped the bedsheet around himself like a toga and swayed slightly, still feeling out of sorts. He made his way over to the wingback chair where his clothes were located and sat with a sigh.

Minerva whisked the heavy drapes open, bathing the room in rich, morning sunlight.

Lively threw his forearm up to his face, shielding his eyes, saying, "Ouch!"

Minerva noted his reaction. "Wow! What's up with you? For a second, I thought you were going to hiss and dissolve into a pile of dust. Are you sure you're okay?"

Slowly taking his arm away from his face, Lively said with a small frown, "I don't know, for some reason this morning, I just feel out of it."

"Well, make sure you let me know when you get back into it, okay?" Minerva stood for a moment admiring the brilliant blue and white day outside. With her room-brightening accomplished, she wandered across to the bathroom door and peeked inside. "Good lord, that's the ugliest bathtub I've ever seen. With claws like that, I hope they keep it on a leash. I wouldn't want to see it roaming the halls around here at night!"

"Tell me about it. But seriously, I want you to promise me something."

"What's that? To never let you pick the flick on movie night? Don't worry, I learned that a long time ago." She shook her head sadly.

"No, that you won't take this place for granted. There's something here that is very oppressive and dangerous. I don't know how else to describe it, but I'm sure you've felt it."

"Don't worry, I'll be careful," she said, then added, "Besides, I've already had my 'Welcome to the Sinclair' experience this morning, anyway."

"Really? What happened?"

She turned back to the room and faced Lively, saying, "Let's just say it was a very expansive experience."

"What? Do you mean to tell me you had a Limey?

"Excuse me, a what?"

"Locational Interdimensional Matter Expansion Experience. Or LIMEE. We call it a Limey for short in the biz."

"Oh, so you're in the 'biz' now, are you? If you mean, did the lobby get really, really big? Then yes, I had a Limey."

"I've heard of that happening but never experienced it," Lively said excitedly.

"Well, let me tell you, it's a very eye-closing experience," Minerva responded, shaking her head slightly.

"Eye-closing?" Lively asked, pulling on his socks. "What do you mean?"

"When a room is expanding around you at a hundred kilometres an hour, it can be very disorienting. Trust me, you need to close your eyes. At least, that's what I did. Then I counted to ten."

"And?"

"And here I am!" Minerva said, doing a quick pirouette.

"I'm serious, Sis, I don't want to lose you to whatever happened to those people in the ballroom." Lively had managed to get his underpants on beneath the bedsheet and was currently working on pulling up his pants.

"It's nice to know you're serious about some things." Minerva looked at her brother's no-nonsense expression and then said, "Okay, fine. I promise to pay close attention and not try anything risky."

"Thank you. And if you want to do a reading, don't do it yourself, that's all I'm asking. Make sure I'm with you, please. I want to be there to pull you back if things get too intense." Lively pulled his pants up the rest of the way and stood, the bedsheet dropping to the floor. He zipped his fly and grabbed for his shirt.

"Yes, sir," Minerva said, giving a weak salute, a small smile playing across the corners of her scarlet-tinted lips. She looked at her brother as he buttoned his shirt. As always, she was impressed with his finely-honed physique. Never a man to work out religiously, he still did his fair share, and it showed. Despite his pushing forty years old, he was in as good a shape as any man half his age. With his dark blonde hair, square jaw and muscular chest, her brother had turned the heads of many people on both sides of the gender spectrum over the years.

Leaving her brother to finish dressing, she wandered back into the main sitting area of the suite, saying, "That's why I stopped over in Vancouver to wait out the storm. I'm not the kind to drive through raging blizzards to get someplace that isn't going anywhere, just to arrive a few hours earlier.

Lively called out as he shrugged into his bomber jacket, "Yeah, it was slow-going on the way up here last night, that's for sure." Taking his courier bag from the dresser next to the suitcase, he slung it over one shoulder and joined his sister in the living area.

Colourful packaging drew Minerva's attention, and she moved to the dusty snack rack near the bar. "By the time I got up here, the highways were all plowed down to some nice hard compact, so I was able to let my Alpina open up her injectors. I bet I made it here in half the time that you did." She picked up a bag of Old Dutch Ripple Chips from the dusty snack rack and tore it open, sniffing the contents delicately for a moment. Wrinkling her nose, a small, "Eww," escaped her lips.

"So, you brought your Winter Warrior with you, did you?"

"Of course! After what I spent, she goes everywhere with me!"

"I'll bet." Lively grinned and nodded slightly, then said, "And now for something completely different, what's for breakfast? I am so hungry! I haven't really eaten since lunch yesterday."

"Well, no wonder you're feeling dizzy and light-headed, you big silly!" She shook her head, hands on her hips.

"I suppose you're right. It might not have been the Barq's bite after all. Well, that is good news since I didn't want to give up my brew. However, I remembered to bring some of my MREs with me if you're interested. They're out in the 4Runner, though, can you give me a hand to bring them inside?"

"Sure. How many did you bring?"

"I brought two cases of US Military-grade MREs and a couple of cases of Russian IRP mountain rations — those are the good ones with the extra chocolate!" Lively added excitedly.

Minerva picked up a King Don and rapped it loudly on the edge of the wire rack for a moment. "Sounds intriguing, but I don't know, they've got some good solid-looking food around here."

"This is true. But I thought it would be best to bring something up here since I presumed the kitchen wouldn't be open." His stomach barked at the mention of open and kitchen in the same sentence. "Plus, these have the meal heaters in them, so we get hot food."

"My, you are the thoughtful one. And I'm sure they cover the full spectrum of nutrients a growing boy like you would need." After a slight pause, she continued, "You said you remembered to bring 'some' of your MREs a moment ago. Please tell me those four cases are the only ones you bought?"

Lively grinned sheepishly at his sister but said nothing.

"You stocked up?" Minerva asked disbelievingly. She unwrapped a Four Flavour bar and saw the only flavour now available was stale, age-bloomed chocolate. She dropped it back on the rack and dusted her fingers, a small grimace on her face.

"Hey," Lively said defensively, "I can have meatloaf any time I want now!"

Minerva shook her head and said, "A million great restaurants in Vancouver and my brother has been eating survival rations." As she spoke, she slung her small, purple bag over one shoulder, then moved toward the door.

In a final futile attempt at justification for his purchase, Lively said, "There are some really tasty entrees with over twelve different menus to choose from, you know. Plus, I had plenty of space in my spare room to boot."

Now standing in the doorway, Minerva asked, "Spare room? How many MREs did you buy?"

"Well, I got a really good deal if I bought them by the pallet." He smiled weakly.

"Sad, just sad." She reached around to the other side of the doorway to the hall, saying, "But that being said, I figured about the same as you, and just in case, I brought a few things of my own along." With a grunt, she dropped a sizeable backpack onto the floor near Lively's feet.

"A few things?"

"A good Scout is always prepared." Minerva held her right hand to her temple in the traditional three-fingered Scout salute.

"You were never a Scout."

"No, but I dated a Scoutmaster several years ago so that almost counts."

Lively shook his head and exited the suite. He stood outside the door and said, "Well, let's get my MREs and then we can have a hot meal in the dining room. Once we're there, you can have a chance to break open the treats in your rucksack, Brunhilda. Here, let me give you a hand." Lively hefted Minerva's backpack and threw it over the shoulder opposite his courier bag, saying, "Holy crap! What do you have in here? It feels like you're ready for the apocalypse!" He began moving slowly down the hallway, pretending to stagger slightly as if under a laborious weight.

Trailing behind Lively, Minerva stuck her tongue out at his back and commented, "Only nuts and berries, of course." As the royal suite receded behind them, she said, "But thanks for playing bellhop, Big Brother. I didn't feel like carrying that pack back down these stairs again."

"You're welcome. But why didn't you leave it in the lobby?"

"Well, after my little Limey experience, I wasn't sure if it would still be there when I got back. I was just happy to see things back to normal when I opened my eyes again. Or as normal as things get around here, at least."

"Good point."

Looking at the closed doors around them as they walked, Minerva asked, "Since you gave yourself the best room in the house, I hope there's something left for me?" They were now about halfway along the hall and approaching a small sitting area.

"I think there's a couple of half-decent rooms left around here. After breakfast, I can talk to the front desk for you, if you like."

"Oh, that would be lovely, Big Brother. It's nice to see you have such pull around here!"

"It's true. I'm in the book, don't you know," Lively stated enigmatically. "But, if you really like the royal suite, I could let you sleep there, and I could switch rooms. I really don't mind."

"That's okay, I prefer something a little more regular person-sized, and not quite as grand as your digs, I think." Minerva's tummy rumbled as they walked down the corridor toward the stairs, and she quickly added, "Well thanks a lot. With all of your talk about food, now I'm ravenous!"

"That's not why. It's driving a BMW at the speed of sound that does that to a person," Lively said with a smile.

Smiling herself, Minerva gave her brother a poke in the ribs for his comment, saying, "I told you I don't speed, I drive fast." They had arrived at the top of the third-floor staircase.

"Uh-huh," Lively shook his head, then looked down the stairs into the cavernous lobby. He flashed back to the night before, adrenaline beginning to course through his veins as he thought of the encounter.

"Over breakfast, remind me to tell you about my new special friend from last night."

"Special friend?" Minerva queried, tilting her head. "Is that what you're calling it now?" She glanced toward Lively's belt buckle. "I don't need every little detail, you know."

Lively noted the direction of her gaze and said, "Ho, ho, very funny. But regarding my friend, trust me, you'll know him if you meet him."

They descended the grand staircase toward the lobby, taking in the decor and architecture as they went. "This staircase looks like it was ripped directly from the Titanic, doesn't it?" Lively asked.

Minerva nodded in agreement, admiring the beautiful rosewood inlay that accented the deep oak balustrades and railings of the grand staircase. Running along one wall as they descended, an art gallery of sorts showed various paintings inspired by the natural beauty that surrounded the hotel.

But there was one painting that particularly caught Minerva's attention, the massive oil painting over the mezzanine. "This one is amazing. I saw it on the way upstairs."

"Called it already."

"What?"

"As soon as I saw it last night, I knew it would be right up your alley, what with your love of Waldo and all."

Looking closer, Minerva could see that in some of the rooms the artist had painted small scenes, or vignettes, depicting patrons of the resort going about their business both inside the hotel and on the grounds that surrounded it. Through one window, larger than the rest, she could see the grand ballroom. Inside, painted in exquisite detail, were dozens of couples dancing to unheard music. Outside on the grounds, several people were depicted playing croquet and sunning themselves near the pool. A small boy and his dog played fetch with a stick next to a dark and forbidding-looking forest.

"Come on, Rembrandt, this isn't the Louvre," Lively said, pulling at the furry sleeve of Minerva's jacket. She ignored him, enraptured by the painting in front of her. Lively spoke again, "Snap out of it, kid! Let's go get some grub."

No longer looking at the painting, but still Ignoring Lively, her nose in the air, Minerva said, "What is that smell? If I didn't know any better, I'd swear I smelled toast."

Lively sniffed but still couldn't smell anything except dust from the circular bed's sheets. Minerva's sense of smell was remarkable, however, and he didn't doubt that she smelled what she said she smelled. But instead, since it was his duty as a big brother, he said, "You know what they say about smelling burnt toast. Maybe it's a brain tumour?"

"It's not a tumour!" Minerva said, doing her best to sound like a certain Austrian preschool police officer.

Lively laughed, saying, "I believe you." He took a deep breath and said, "But now that you mention it, you're right, I can smell it, too."

"I think the odds of us both having a tumour at the same time is a bit of a longshot." She sniffed again, then added, "And I think I smell bacon, too!"

Arriving on the main floor, Lively said, "I concur," as he sniffed the air. He spied the doors to the main dining room across the lobby next to the lounge and popped his head through, taking a deep breath. He was disappointed to only smell dust and stale, uncirculated air.

"Lively!" Minerva called from across the lobby.

"What is it, Sis?"

"The toast smell is coming from the basement," she said, pointing down a utility staircase located off to one side of the front desk.

"That's right, the kitchen is located down there."

"So, someone cooked us breakfast? Who else is here?" Side by side, they slowly descended the stairs to the basement.

"No one, we're the first people to have entered this building in almost forty years." Lively replied.

Minerva nodded and added, "Or, maybe there's somebody around here who never left."

CHAPTER TWELVE

January 2nd, 1982 0115 hours

The single fifteen-watt bulb over the stovetop spotlighted a piece of notepaper, tented in the middle, sitting beneath. John's name was written on the front in a graceful feminine hand. He read the note and smiled, a single tear tracing down one cheek as he did. Another chance to have a holiday together with his wife was now gone because of work, like so many holidays, over so many years before. He longed for them to have the time together, but his job took priority. Fortunately, Helen understood that though his duties took him away from her, she was always in his heart.

A foil-wrapped plate waited patiently inside the oven for him. John didn't realise how hungry he was until he began eating. The scalloped potatoes were drying at the edges, and the ham had started approaching jerky territory, but he didn't care, he was starving. On a second plate in the middle of the kitchen table, Helen had left a large slice of caramel pecan pie covered in plastic wrap. Grabbing the dinner fork from his plate, he retreated with his plasticised pie to the den. He needed to do some research.

Through the miracle of modern technology, the 300 baud dial-up modem on John Harder's brand-new Texas Instruments TI-99/4A personal computer allowed him remote access to the recently formed RCMP informational database. Though it cut into sleep he sorely needed, he wanted to know more about the Sinclair empire.

The hotel had been named after the man that built it, Thomas Sinclair. A transplanted Scotsman, he'd moved to Canada in the early 1890s, making his fortune in land, lumber and other people's vices. He'd made nothing but money for the next five decades, becoming one of the wealthiest men in Canada and also the world. Unfortunately, he attained the latter lofty title only just a few months before he passed away.

Sinclair's fortune had gotten its start in a remote West-Kootenay community that had built up around a small trading post. When gold was struck in the area, the settlement mushroomed into a bustling burg of almost twelve-thousand souls within less than one year. Affectionately nicknamed for what the area became after the gold strike, the name stuck and the town of Lawless, BC, was born. A rough and tumble town where, if you didn't keep one hand on your gold and the other on a loaded gun, you'd be apt to lose both if you weren't careful.

Thomas Sinclair fit right into the mayhem. He was a mean Scottish drunk with a keen business sense, and also a man proud of his heritage. Whenever someone called him 'Scotch', he was purported to have loudly corrected the misinformed soul and say, "Scotch is a drink! Not a goddamned people!"

The Sinclair name became synonymous with posh digs. Any miner who struck the motherlode could afford to stay at one of Sinclair's luxurious establishments, but not for long, thanks to their exorbitant rates. Fine food and finer drink were only part of what was offered, however. In conjunction with bars and inns, another money-making aspect of Sinclair Enterprises had been its brothels, which sprang up wherever there was a gold strike. Company of the softer and curvier variety was something that many a lonely miner desired, and Sinclair was more than happy to provide it. The wiley Scotsman, it was said, could provide your most intimate desire, no matter what it was, but chances were you wouldn't like some of the long-term strings attached.

The opportunities for a man that provided vices like Sinclair were immense. For default on payment for services rendered or gambling debts incurred, he'd acquired vast tracts of land along with the deeds to many mines over the years.

John was stunned by the amounts of money that a man could squander, and the depths to which another man, Sinclair, would go to swindle the first man by charging inflated prices for his products and services.

At the height of the Yukon's rush in 1896, it was reported that one wayward gold miner had spent almost thirty-thousand dollars in a single evening at one of Sinclair's hotels (which would be somewhere in the vicinity of a quarter-million dollars in 1982, John calculated). A single sixty-dollar magnum of champagne back then would cost the equivalent of five-hundred dollars today. So, it wasn't hard for a miner to blow through six months worth of hard gold-mining labour in a single evening, with Thomas Sinclair standing by, ready to collect. When a miner ran out of gold, and found themselves in dire straits, to settle their debt, most opted to hand over the deed to their land, house, or both. Those who needed some persuasion got to speak directly to Sinclair's right (and left) hand men. And for those that would not listen to reason, or refused to pay, they were rumoured to have paid the ultimate price.

Sinclair married Margarethe Hoffman in 1901, and they settled down in Vancouver, British Columbia. Margarethe gave birth to two sons, Edward in 1907 and Matthew in 1913. Both attended Vancouver's finest schools, and both had significant behavioural problems, not unlike their father.

The millions of acres acquired legally, and sometimes illegally by the Sinclair Corporation was a definite boon to a person like Matthew Sinclair. Straight out of business school, he began to manage the dozens of Sinclair owned saw and pulp mills up and down the West Coast. And he embezzled millions upon millions of dollars from them in the process. Matthew was also a gambler, womaniser and raging alcoholic — not a good combination. Late one October night in 1938, an estranged husband of a woman with whom he was having an affair put five bullet holes in his chest.

Edward Sinclair was a brilliant engineer and architect. He took over the family construction business once he'd completed university at UBC. Several landmark hotel and office buildings around Vancouver in the late 1930s and early 1940s were designed by him and built by the Sinclair Construction Group. Unlike his brother, he was a very private man who, though never married, had been linked to several high-profile Hollywood actresses in the 1940s and 1950s.

Thomas Sinclair's health began fading near the end of World War II, and it was at this time he decided he needed to build something that would stand as a monument to himself. Something magnificent, iconic, and grand that would survive the test of time, like the Pyramids of Giza or Mount

Rushmore. Harnessing Edward's architectural genius, Thomas crafted plans for a massive resort in the interior of British Columbia, something grand, yet remote. A place where the rich and elite of the world could come to relax and get away from it all.

On October 31st, 1945, construction broke ground at the Sinclair Resort Hotel. Despite his vast fortune, there was one thing of which Thomas Sinclair could not buy any more — time. He was eighty-five years old when the construction began, and the practical Scotsman knew that his own remaining time was short. So, with money no object, the construction of the resort had been expedited.

Numerous shipping containers were delivered to the site on a regular basis from Sinclair's native Scotland. Inside them, pieces of a family castle were brought over stone by stone for almost fourteen months. Over fifty percent of the resort's main building consisted of various bits and pieces of the dismembered castle.

Forever in the shadow of the Sinclair's mountaintop perch, Entwistle, BC, languished, the victim of a silver rush gone bust many years before. A work camp was set up on the town's outskirts, where the workers stayed and lived for the next year as the resort was constructed. In rotating twelve-hour shifts, the men were shuttled up and down the mountain, twenty-four hours a day, seven days a week. Though a canteen was provided on the camp's site, when a man happened to get a day off, hungry and thirsty, they inevitably came into Entwistle. The small town responded to them, embracing the new business opportunities the worker's appetites brought with them.

For the final few months, as the resort's interior was being completed, they had all been laid off. A large group of Freemasons, of which Sinclair was a member, had come to the resort. For the final three months of construction, they worked around the clock, finishing off the interior. Local carpenters, plumbers and stonemasons had also been involved in the initial build, but they had been laid off as well. No one was able to say for sure what sort of interior construction had occurred in that time. Then, mysteriously as they arrived, the Freemasons left all at once, just before the hotel started to bring in the furnishings, decorations and appliances.

The last stone was set in place just before Christmas, 1946. A week later, on December 31st, the Sinclair Resort opened to the world and held an inaugural New Year's Eve party. It was a resounding success with celebrities and royalty attending from all over North America and Europe. That night, the grand ballroom and both of the secondary ballrooms were filled to capacity. Over five-hundred guests flocked to the resort to drink, dine and dance the night away at the party of the century.

Thomas Sinclair passed away the next morning, on New Year's day, 1947. Edward was said to have found his lifeless body sprawled atop the bed in the hotel's royal suite. It appeared as if he'd come upstairs, too tired to undress, then lay down fully clothed on the bed and proceeded to die. Some thought it happened then because he knew he could finally rest, knowing he was memorialised forever by the hotel, while others said it was due to exhaustion. Whatever the cause, he was eventually buried in a mausoleum rumoured to be located somewhere on the resort property.

Much like Entwistle in the shadow of Overseer Mountain, Edward had struggled against his father's domination for many, many years. But after Thomas's death, he had been able to invest his time in other pursuits, some more legally questionable than others. In addition to these new pursuits, he'd continued to run the Sinclair Corporation quite successfully, with the resort being his personal pride and joy, just like it had been for his father.

It was said that Edward 'took care of things' up on the Hill, as the resort was known down in town. Palms were greased when they needed it, and any little 'embarrassments' at the resort were covered up or disposed of as quickly as possible. Though his father had some powerful friends in high places throughout the world, Edward, on the other hand, had equally powerful and dangerous friends in low places. Over the years, he had been personally connected to several high-profile members of the Gambino crime family in New York along with other questionable acquaintances from Las Vegas.

Throughout the '50s and ' 60s, the hotel was the site of many high-profile dinners and balls for royalty, political dignitaries, and the entertainment industry. The West Coast Movie and Television Award Dinner and Dance was, in fact, the longest-running event at the resort since being first held there on December 31st, 1963. John found it exceedingly strange that the first and last events held for that group also had tragedy attached to them with the suicide of one of the staff that same week, along with one of the hotel's first missing person cases. Harder had been new to the Entwistle detachment at the time and had only been peripherally involved in the investigation. But even that case involved many unanswered questions even now after all these years.

The most recent dinner and dance last night was also a celebration of the continued success of the entertainment industry over the previous year, as well as a look ahead to the future. Word had spread at the resort that a special surprise was also being planned by Edward Sinclair for the midnight celebration. Unfortunately, he was the only person who knew what it was, and he had vanished, along with everyone else in that room, when the clock struck midnight on December 31st.

"Hmmph," John muttered to himself quietly, "I wonder if the surprise was the disappearance of everyone in the ballroom?"

John clicked off his computer and rubbed his eyes. It was four minutes past two in the morning, and he was officially exhausted. He stumbled sleepily to bed and crawled in next to Helen, who was snoring lightly. His mind was awhirl with images of construction, corruption, and celebration. When he finally tumbled into sleep, it was dark and troubled, the Sinclair Hotel now haunting his nights as well as his days.

CHAPTER THIRTEEN

December 24th, 2021 0755 hours

The scent of freshly ground coffee lingered in the air of the kitchen, blending with the aroma of toasted bread. Industrial stainless-steel countertops dotted the gleaming room. Along the far wall sat three equally stainless-steel stovetops with large ovens beneath. And in keeping with the resort's overarching theme, all the equipment appeared to be electrical, which was rare in an industrial kitchen, especially one in a hotel.

"What the hell?" Lively said, entering the room first. It was spotless, without a trace of dust anywhere, and everything gleamed as if freshly polished. He turned around in a circle taking it all in. "You can always judge a joint by the cleanliness of its kitchen, they say."

"They also say it's the heart of a home, but I don't know if that applies to this place," Minerva added, entering the room behind Lively.

"Yeah, I think it could use a cardiac bypass with all the bizarre stuff that happened around here."

"Well, it looks like the last forty years have bypassed this room, that's for sure." Minerva looked down at the shiny, industrial grey floor and added, "You could eat off the linoleum in here!" She shook her head in amazement.

In the middle of the room sat a large gleaming island covered with enticing looking food items. On one end sat two stacks of buttered toast, one white and one whole wheat. Beside them, sitting on a small hotplate, was a glass pot that read 'Bunn' on the side. It was filled with hot coffee, steam swirling from its top. A silver serving dish filled with back bacon that looked crispy and chewy in all the right spots sat beside a large crock of strawberry jam. Nearby, two small bears relaxed on the label of a clear glass jar. Next to the counter, a row of stainless-steel stools sat empty, pulled out just a little as if waiting for someone to occupy them.

With a deep inhale, Lively savoured the heady scent of coffee, bacon and toast all blending together. "It smells amazing in here!" He scanned what was on the table for a moment, then grabbed two slices of toast from the white stack. One piece was slathered with a gooey knifeful of peanut butter, the other with a liberal dollop of jam. With a satisfied nod, Lively slapped the two sandwich halves together and took a large bite.

"Lively! What are you doing? We don't know that this stuff is safe!" Minerva said, surprised to see him being so bold.

Munching on his mouthful of toast for a moment, Lively held up his right index finger and said, "Well, first of all, I'm starving." He took another large bite of sandwich. After another couple of powerful chews, he made a large swallow and held up his middle finger, forming the peace sign. "And second of all, this is delicious." He paused and chewed for several more seconds, apparently having not quite worked his way through all of the peanut butter yet. Then he continued, "The way I see it, if the Sinclair wanted us dead, it would have killed us already." Lively picked up the coffee pot as he spoke and poured two cups of steaming coffee. He placed one in front of Minerva, black just like she liked it. "I mean, why go to all the trouble to have this appear for us if it could have done away with me last night and finished you off as soon as you stepped through the front doors this morning?"

"So, you think the hotel was only playing with me in the lobby? Sort of trying to test my mettle, huh?" Minerva blew on her cup and took a tentative sip of the hot coffee.

"To see what we're made of. Yeah, for the moment I think that's what it's doing. Kind of testing us, looking for our weaknesses, but that might be subject to change at any time, so be on your guard," Lively said, pouring cream from a tall silver decanter into his coffee. It was so thick compared to the half and half he used back home and the colour much more golden, like pouring liquid butter. On his first sip of the hot brew, his taste buds came alive, and they pronounced it 'delicious'. He made a pleasurable, "Ah!" then took another sip. Smacking his lips together, Lively added, "I can't remember the last time I had a cup of coffee that tasted so fresh and full-bodied." He half-expected to see Mrs. Olson pop out of a pantry door across the room, grinning brightly, a jar of Folger's finest proudly displayed in one hand.

As that thought entered his head, a flashback to last night suddenly played on the 8K widescreen behind Lively's eyes. He remembered looking into the mirror in the royal suite, but that had been it, until now. Now, he remembered something more — not a lot, but more. A sudden series of images flashed through his mind: the lobby, blackness, shining metal everywhere, and finally, a reflection of himself again, standing next to a series of glass shelves in front of a large mirror somewhere inside the hotel. In the mirror, his likeness still grinned like all of its oars weren't paddling in the same direction, followed by more blackness.

He still hadn't said anything to Minerva about what happened with the mirror before he 'went to bed' last night. He wasn't sure what to make of it and decided to observe his behaviour for a while. Lively reasoned if he saw or felt anything out of the ordinary, he would let his sister know. But then another little voice inside his head wondered, what if he lost that piece of himself somewhere inside this hotel? The piece of him that was aware enough to seek help? Or would it be too late by then?

"My, it looks like the gears are grinding away in there. I'm surprised not to see smoke pouring out of your ears!" Minerva said, studying Lively's expression.

Lively came back to the world, giving his head a slight shake. "Sorry, just thinking some thoughts."

"Anything you'd like to share?"

"Not right at the moment. I'll keep you posted."

"Well, make sure you do. I think around this place, the smallest detail could make the biggest difference in whether we can figure this out, or not. Remember, sharing is caring!"

"Yes, mother," Lively said, smiling. As those words exited his mouth, he received a piece of toast crust Minerva had torn off of a slice and expertly flicked into his coffee cup in return.

"Hey! I'm not done yet!" Lively fished the bread crust out of his cup and took a gulp of coffee. He held his sandwich in the other hand and took another huge bite, almost succeeding in jamming the entire thing into his mouth. He munched for several seconds. "Wow, that is really, really good. But who do we have to thank for it?" He looked around the kitchen but saw no one in sight.

Minerva shook her head and took another sip from her cup of coffee now that it had cooled a moment. The brew was full-bodied and rich, and she thought she detected notes of dark chocolate. With a small smack of her lips, she said, "Ricardo Montalban would be proud."

"Good to the last drop, isn't it?"

Minerva nodded. She took the crustless piece of toast she held and spread a thin layer of jam on top. After nibbling delicately on the corner for a moment, she added, "And good to the last crust, because you're right, this is delicious. It's like when you're high, and you have some post-blunt snack that tastes just amazing because you have the munchies."

"Well, speak for yourself," Lively said, shaking his head. "I was part of the establishment, remember? The Man? CSIS? I was recruited young, and I was regularly tested for drugs because of my job level. So, I never had the opportunity, or wanted, to have anything more mind-altering than Moosehead or Barq's."

"Just two beers, huh? One alcoholic, and one not. Hmm... How boring." Minerva took another small bite of toast, and a dribble of strawberry jam ran down onto her fingers. She licked the sticky coating from her digits, then pulled the jar of peanut butter across the countertop toward herself, studying its label a bit more closely. She stopped chewing abruptly, a frown creasing her brow.

Lively observed this and asked, "Speaking of grinding gears, what's the matter?"

"Well, nothing, I think, but I was just looking at this jar, and I haven't seen one that looked like this before." She slid it toward him across the stainless-steel tabletop. It spun like a puck on ice.

Lively grabbed for it just before it sailed off the edge to its doom. He examined the green foil label. A pair of twin, blonde bear cubs relaxed on the front, declaring it to be a jar of Kraft Peanut Butter. But the label looked all wrong, like something from the fifties or sixties. Not to mention it was made of glass, not PETE plastic as most peanut butter jars were these days.

"The weight on the label says eighteen ounces, not five-hundred grams, or whatever they weigh these days. I wonder if it's American?" He turned it around in his hands. "Nope, says 'Made in Canada'. Hey, there's an expiry date on it." His eyes widened as he read it. "Where in the heck did they get this jar?"

"How long ago did it expire?"

"December 1963."

Smiling, Minerva said, "Glad I chose the jam."

"Well, I think it must be the mountain air. Keeps things fresh longer. And makes everything taste better, too, even expired food." Lively loaded up another couple of slices of toast with peanut butter, then threw in several pieces of bacon, skipping the jam altogether. He took a big bite, and a look of bliss crossed his face.

Minerva cringed slightly as she watched her brother partake of his latest creation.

After a moment of chewing, Lively saw Minerva's expression and said, "Hey, look it up! It's a thing. And it's delicious!"

Minerva did not look convinced. Around another delicate bite of toast, she said, "I'll take your word for it. So, what's on the agenda for today, Big Brother?"

Pulling a linen napkin from a stack in the middle of the table, Lively said, "First thing we need to do today, as I see it, is to scope out the hotel, just to verify we're the only ones here." He wiped some bacon grease and peanut butter from the corner of his mouth with the napkin. "As far as I know, this building has remained sealed for almost forty years now.

"So was this area, supposedly. But it's so clean in here it looks like they're ready to start serving guests at any minute." Minerva ran her finger along the surface of the table and then examined it. It was completely dust-free.

"Say, who is this cryptic new special friend you mentioned earlier?"

"Oh, you mean Thumper?"

"Thumper? Like Bambi's friend? Are you sure you don't mean Harvey?" Minerva asked, a small smile playing at the corners of her lips.

"Ha, ha. No, I did not see a six-foot tall rabbit like Elwood P. Dowd did, but thanks for asking."

"Actually, Harvey was a Pooka, and he was six feet, three and a half inches tall," Minerva corrected, still nibbling away. "And they can supposedly appear as anything they want, anyway, not just a rabbit you know."

"Well, Pookas are Irish, and the parts of the castle that Sinclair brought over were from Scotland, not Ireland. So, I guess it can't be a Pooka."

"Sure it can! The Gael's mythology influenced almost all of the United Kingdom, as you know. Most of that part of the world's Celtic folklore shares variations of those same legends." Minerva finished her toast and had a large gulp of her rapidly cooling coffee. "I mean, look at the Kelpie in Scotland. It's very similar."

"Well, thank you, Professor History," Lively said, smiling. Minerva stuck her tongue out at him in response. He continued, "So, it's possible that when Sinclair moved that castle from Scotland over to here, either by accident or intentionally, and this Pooka..."

"Or Kelpie," Minerva interjected.

"Or Kelpie," Lively nodded with a smile, then continued, "came along for the ride and it got incorporated into this hotel. But how does that play into the disappearance, I wonder? Are they related?"

"That's why we're here. To figure this out." Now finished with her coffee and toast, Minerva stood and wandered briefly around the kitchen looking at the appliances and peeking inside the ovens. A short corridor led to a series of latched cooler and freezer doors. She peered inside each one, but all were empty. "Well, I don't know where the food came from for our breakfast, since Old Mother Hubbard's cupboards are bare at the moment."

Lively walked up behind her, still wiping crumbs from the corners of his mouth. "Not surprising, I didn't expect you'd find anything."

"What? Why?"

"I have a theory, but I am going to hold off on sharing it for the moment."

"That's not playing fair! You need to tell me what it is," Minerva said with a small pout.

"Very soon, but I want to verify a few things first. Let me just say this for now; our reality here in this hotel is, quite possibly, not the only one."

"Multiple realities coexisting here at the same time and interacting with each other? Sure, why not?" Minerva asked facetiously as she closed the final pantry door at the end of the short hall.

"I'm glad you're on board with the concept," Lively said with a grin. "Shall we make like a leaf and blow?"

"Absolutely! But the first place I'd like to gust toward is the ballroom!"

"You read my mind, Sis."

"Don't I always?"

"No, not always. I bet you can't think of what else I'm thinking right now."

"You're thinking of meatloaf and want to bring in your MREs," Minerva said.

"Lucky guess." Lively mock-scowled at her.

Now at the door, Minerva smiled sweetly at Lively, then turned and called back into the empty kitchen, "Thanks for the breakfast, Mystery Chef! For lunch, I'd like macaroni and cheese!"

Lively shook his head and said nothing, moving down the corridor to the stairs. As he walked, he saw there were many more rooms in the basement that would require exploration, in addition to the suites and other areas. But the ballroom was key to everything that happened here, or so he believed, and he was excited to go there first. As his high-top sneakers slapped up the carpeted stairs, he noted that the dust clouds formed by his footfalls were much less dense than they had been the night before when he'd climbed the main staircase. While not as spotless as the kitchen, it was definitely cleaner. He paused for a moment on a short dogleg in the stairs about halfway up and stamped his feet on the carpet a few times to verify.

With the sound of boot heels tapping up the carpeted stairs at his back, Minerva said, "Aww, what's the matter, didn't you get your way?"

"Hardy-har-har, you're too funny. Actually, I just noticed something."

"Thank you, I'll be here all week." Minerva grinned, then looked down at Lively's feet and asked, "Okay, what did you notice? That your footwear is seriously out of style?"

"Hey, that's retro fashion, I'll have you know." He looked back down at his feet and said, "While I realise it's the maid's day off around here, I think these steps look a little cleaner all of a sudden as well, don't you think?"

"Well, maybe what happened in the kitchen is spreading from the basement throughout the hotel? I don't know for sure, but things certainly do seem to be happening around here since we've arrived."

"I know, it's like now that we're here, the hotel is waking up after decades of dormancy," Lively added quietly, still lost in thought.

"So, you think our timer has started ticking?"

He turned to Minerva, a grave look on his face, and said, "That it is. And I think our time is running out.

CHAPTER FOURTEEN

January 2nd, 1982 0605 hours

Tossing and turning, John had eventually fallen into a restless sleep, punctuated by dreams of a ballroom full of revellers spinning and swaying to an unheard orchestra, forever dancing, and never, ever stopping.

John snapped awake with that image in his head, then lay staring at the ceiling for what felt like a long time.

'Snick'. The analogue clock radio on the night table next to his head flipped the next digit over on its display.

With bleary eyes, John stared at the clock face for several seconds. It was now 6:05 A.M. As he watched, a number six plopped down on the right side, where only moments before it seemed the five had been revealed.

No matter how far past his bedtime when he went to bed the night before, John's internal clock awoke him, rain or shine, just about six o'clock every morning, seven days a week. After his late-night research, he felt informed but groggy. When sitting down at the computer last night, he knew he'd have to pay the price this morning. He smiled and mentally chided himself, 'last night' and 'this morning' were still the same day, only four hours later. It was always surprising to him how a brief break in one's consciousness made it feel like a new day had started, even though you knew better. But he'd had similarly long nights before, and in his experience, it wasn't anything that a hot cup of coffee or three couldn't cure.

John closed his eyes again for a brief moment before getting out of bed. Lying there, he enjoyed the cocoon-like warmth of the heavy blankets over the two of them, and almost fell asleep again. But The Sinclair was already gnawing away at his mind, needing to be investigated and solved. And yet, he paused a moment longer, relishing the feeling of his wife's warm body next to his, snoring ever so gently. Before creeping from between the covers, John tenderly kissed Helen's forehead, and his heart broke. A slight smile played around one corner of her beautiful mouth, and he felt a pang of guilt, knowing they would have to spend yet another day apart. With a faint smile, he placated himself with the thought of his retirement coming up in the next five years. Once he made it to that point, he would have plenty of time to make up for his previous absences in Helen's life, of that he was sure.

As he dressed, he mulled his experience in the ballroom over and over in his head. It all felt like a jumble. What he'd thought he'd seen in the mirror had to have been caused by exhaustion — his mind playing tricks on him. He was an open-minded man, but what he thought he'd witnessed last night was stretching things to his mental limit.

The automatic timer on the Mr. Coffee machine clicked off just as John walked into the kitchen. With several small plops, the last few drops of liquid dripped from its filter basket into the carafe below. "Perfect timing," he said, inhaling deeply of the caffeinated air. He grabbed the pot while the final few drops dripped, and they sizzled loudly as they hit the warming element. After pouring two-thirds of the carafe into his massive travel mug, John slid the pot back onto the still sputtering element. With a huge splash of cream and a quick stir, he took several satisfied slurps of his first bracing brew of the day.

John was a creature of habit, always transcribing his day's shorthand notes and audio recordings into a journal each evening. Except for last night, he had been far too tired after his research. He hoped to catch up later this afternoon if he got a chance. Someday soon he would have to forgo this old-fashioned paper trail and begin typing his notes into his new computer, saving them for posterity on its five and a quarter inch disk drive — very high tech indeed. He shook his head, marvelling at the thought and smiling slightly. The way things were going these days, soon he'd be using optical data cubes or some such thing like on Star Trek to store his data.

Stepping outside his front door, John embraced the chill of the new day. His Suburban's windshield was thick with frost after sitting for less than six hours. The day was crisp and clear, with a cold wind that nipped at his nose and cheeks. Fortunately, his head and ears were quite toasty, thanks to the winter-issue RCMP muskrat fur hat on his head. While he waited for the Chevy Suburban to warm up before heading back up the mountain, he pulled his microcassette recorder from his briefcase. He wanted to listen to the second tape recording of his interview with the bartender who'd been covering the ballroom during the evening of the disappearance, James O'Malley.

Harder also wanted to examine the mysterious box in the ballroom further today and knew that the bartender had had some involvement with it, due to his own admissions. It had been a very interesting conversation to be sure, but especially so now, in light of his own experience in the ballroom last night. He needed to hear the man tell his tale again. So much more could be gleaned listening to a person talk rather than reading a transcript of a conversation. With a blow into the microphone, John heard his own recorded voice as he began O'Malley's interview.

***

"This is the second interview with Mr. James O'Malley, conducted by John Harder, January 1st, 1982. Mr. O'Malley, please continue with your recounting of the events in the Snowdrop Lounge on December 24th, 1981."

"Sure, okay. Well, the Drop, that's what we call the Snowdrop Lounge around here, had been really quiet that night. After I'd only served about four customers in four hours, I decided that since Judy, the waitress, didn't have much to do, there wasn't much point in having two people on when it was so slow, so I sent her home. It's usually my call like that if it's quiet. Being Christmas Eve and all, Judy didn't mind getting off early, let me tell you. I've never seen her smile so much! And anyway, I'd heard the storm was going to pick up, so I thought it best to let her off early because of that as well. Anyway, she was out of here by about seven o'clock and heading back down the mountain.

So, that left me standing behind the bar, looking at Baldwin over at the front desk. I tell you, he looked as bored as I felt. It's company policy to leave the door to the lounge open, and I didn't mind, even during the winter like this it's really not too drafty. I tell you, the baseboard heater at my back always feels nice and toasty as I stand back here and serve drinks to people.

The usual Christmas rush wasn't happening this year like it normally was. I think that winter storm slamming the coast scared a lot of customers away. Not as many people travelling for pleasure when it's shitty outside like that, pardon my French. The road up to this resort is treacherous at the best of times. I think the front desk had only seen a half-dozen guests for the whole day.

Even though the lounge doesn't close down until midnight, I like to get a head start on my clean-up when it gets to be a little after eleven. But it had been so quiet that night that I had everything pretty much already done by ten o'clock! I'd been thinking to myself that this shift had to be one of the most boring ones in recent memory, but boy was I wrong.

Around a quarter after eleven, I was busy wiping the spots off of some wine glasses with my back to the lounge, since like I said, I had nothing better to do. I could see the whole room at my back in the mirror, and there was nobody anywhere in sight. But all of a sudden, there was the sound of bar stool legs scraping on the floor behind me. Made me jump a little. Now, as I said, I'd been keeping an eye on the mirror, and I couldn't figure out how anyone could sneak up on me like that. I'm usually on top of things. Must have been tired, I figured.

So, I turned around, and there's this skinny older guy in a black pin-striped suit, with a bowler hat on his head. You know the kind of hat I mean? Like John Steed wears on that British show, The Avengers? And he was wearing a red silk tie that had a huge diamond stickpin in the middle of it. I remember thinking that if that thing were real, it'd be worth more than an entire year of my wages, so I could see this guy had money. But man, he was pale. Looked like he hadn't seen much daylight over the last little while. But then again, who has, right? What with the clouds and snow we've had over the last few weeks up here? I heard it was so bad that they had to shut the road down about nine o'clock, just a couple hours after Judy left. I kinda wondered since that was the case, how'd he get up here then? Snowmobile? Dog sled?

Anyway, I say to him, "Evening, sir, can I get you something?"

He doesn't say anything for a moment and just stares at me like he was sizing me up for something, you know?

Let me tell you, I was starting to get pretty uncomfortable by the time he finally did speak, and then he says, all solemn-like, "I'll take two shots of Glenfiddich, Private Vintage, Single malt. Oh, and add a half-dozen drops of water if you would, my good man."

"Yes, sir! Right away, sir," I said. The bottle of 1958 Private Vintage Glenfiddich Scotch Whisky is the most expensive scotch we carry. Just one single ounce costs two hundred dollars! So, two shots were a big sale, especially after how slow it had been! I grabbed the bottle from the top shelf and carefully measured out the right amount. The management around here is very picky about how the pricey booze is handled and makes us keep strict track of the sales from the bottles. I suppose it's just in case a member of the staff took a liking to something that was way out of their price range and started helping themselves. As soon as I poured the drinks, I had to note it in the logbook sitting underneath the bottle.

But it was weird what happened next. Get this, I'm pouring the second shot, and I glance up into the mirror, and all of a sudden, I thought the guy had left, skipping out after making the order or something. Well, when I turned, I was so surprised, I almost spilled the shots. Cause there the guy sat, looking all regal-like on his stool. I figured maybe it was just the lights here in the Drop playing tricks on my eyes. I mean, you can see how friggin' dim it is in here, right? You almost need a flashlight for Pete's sake!

So, he's sitting there, and he gives me this big smile all full of crooked teeth, and once he sees he has my attention, he begins peeling the skin off his hands! At least, that's what I thought at first. Turns out he's wearing these thin leather gloves, really light coloured, almost like the colour of human skin. That was very weird. But let me tell you, that smile of his was worse. For a person with his kind of money, I figured he would have at least gotten around to getting his teeth fixed by that stage of his life, you know? Swear to God, he looked like Count Chocula from my kid's breakfast cereal box.

Anyway, I slide the shots across the bar on a linen napkin, and the Count picks one up. He sips it all delicate-like, then makes a little, appreciative, "Ah," and sips a bit more. And then he says, "That is the nectar of the Gods, my friend."

"Yessir, it's a very rare blend," I say, then add, "But we don't have too many people ever asking for it."

"Only those with refined and cultured palates, I assume."

"Right, that and a thick wallet."

The guy laughed at that, and he smiled with all those teeth again. And then he slides one of the shot glasses across the bar toward me, saying, "Join me, please."

I said, "I'm really not supposed to drink with the guests while on duty, sir." Then, I pushed the glass back toward him.

"I'm sure that's something your employer would frown upon, but seeing as it's almost closing time, what could it hurt?" He looked sneakily around the room and smiled, saying, "I don't see anyone else around that could object. And besides, how often do you get the chance to take a glass of scotch like this out for a test drive?"

"Well, never, really," I admitted.

Then he slides the glass over to my side again, saying, "Go ahead, my fine friend, enjoy!"

I looked around, saw nobody was watching, and I had a quick sip of the expensive hooch. I tell you, that stuff didn't burn its way down like some of the cheaper stuff we sell in this joint. It was warm, smooth, and mellow, just a touch of sweetness — tasted like money, you know? I rolled it around in my mouth and let my taste buds have a little party for a second. I could see why this cost so much. Before I knew it, I had the last of the scotch in my mouth and finished it off in a quick gulp.

The Count laughed and smiled, saying, "It's always wonderful to see someone not accustomed to the finer things in life, finally getting a chance to sample them."

I nodded back at him, still feeling that stuff warming me all the way down to my toes.

"I'm wondering if you could do me a favour, though."

So, I wiped the back of my hand across my mouth and kinda sighed inside. I should have figured there'd be a catch.

Knowing I was on the hook for the two-hundred-dollar shot now, I said, "I'll do my best to accommodate you, sir."

"Splendid! I have something I'd like to leave for a friend who won't be here until New Year's eve next week. Is there a chance I could leave it here with you? That is if you were going to be travailing on the eve of the grand event yourself, that is?"

Travail on the eve of the grand event? What the hell is this guy talking about? Is he even speaking English, I wonder? Some people and their two-dollar words, I tell you. Anyway, I say, "I'm sorry, sir?"

He clarifies things for me, saying, "Why, working during the New Year's Eve gala in the ballroom, of course, my fine friend! I was hoping you might be on shift that evening?" The Count bends down at this point and picks up a black doctor's bag at his feet and sits it on the stool next to him.

"Yes sir, I'll be working in the ballroom, unfortunately."

"Why, unfortunately?"

Well, it must have been the booze loosening my tongue a bit because I vented a little at him while he dug around in his bag. I said, "It's always a grind, serving all the rich and famous types and watching them have a grand old time. While there I am, standing behind the bar and smiling like I wouldn't rather be any other place than right there on New Year's eve. But, hey, at least the tips are okay that night."

"I'm sure they are. And I promise you, this upcoming New Year's eve will be an evening to remember for the rest of your life!" He reaches into his bag and pulls out this small dark box, about a foot tall. He says, "Tell you what, I'll leave this with you, and if you can place it out on the end of the bar in the grand ballroom around eleven o'clock, an acquaintance of mine will stop by just around midnight to pick it up, and nobody will be the wiser."

"I suppose I could do that," I say. "What does this guy look like?"

"Don't worry about that, just leave it on the far end of the bar. Let me just say this, you'll know him when you meet him, all right?"

"Yessir," I nodded, then said, "Should I ask what's in it?"

"You should more correctly ask, what will be in it!" The Count smiles again and lets out this god-awful little laugh.

So, I say, "Look, I really appreciate the drink and all, but I don't think I should be doing this and acting as a go-between for you and your friend. I mean, there's nothing illegal in that box, is there?"

He chuckles to himself, reaches into his pocket and pulls out a wad of cash you could choke at least two horses with! You know what I mean? It was huge! So, he peels off a bill, slaps it on the bar and slides it across to me, saying, "I believe this should cover tonight's festivities and I'd like you to keep the change for your troubles next week."

At first, all I see is a number one in each corner of the bill, so I think it's an old dollar bill. But then, I see the three zeros after the one, and I realise it's a thousand bucks! I mean, who pays for their drinks with a thousand-dollar bill? Even after taking the four-hundred dollars to cover the cost of two scotches, that would leave over six hundred bucks for me as a tip! Something that would come in very handy over Christmas, let me tell you. So, I say, "All right, sir, I think we have a deal."

"Thank you, young man, your assistance in this matter is greatly appreciated!" So, he walks away a few steps, then turns around and says, "One final thing, though."

"Yes sir? What's that?"

"Do not open this box or try to open it. If you do, my acquaintance will know if you've tampered with it, and he will become very distraught, shall we say? And trust me when I tell you, you don't want to make him distraught."

"You can count on me, sir," I said, feeling a little freaked out by that comment. Who was this friend of his?

"Excellent! That's what I was hoping you'd say. Thank you, my fine young friend. A good evening to you." So, he turns to leave and starts hustling toward the door, and then I see that he didn't finish his drink and call out, "What about the rest of your whiskey, sir?"

The Count was already walking toward the door of the lounge at a pretty fast clip when I spoke, so I guess he couldn't hear me, cause he kept on going. Not wanting anything to go to waste, I pick up his glass, and turn toward the shelves and the mirror again to hide my final big slurp of the remaining scotch. I know what you're thinking, but waste not, want not, that's what my mom always used to say.

So, after I downed the booze, I turned back to grab the box from the bar and was surprised to see the guy is still in the doorway to the lounge, looking in at me. I smile at him, and he tips his bowler at me. Then he turns and walks toward the front desk. I pick up the box and place it on the back side of the bar, up against the mirror. When I glanced into the mirror again, he was gone. What the hell? I thought he was going to the front desk. Strange, I think, but maybe he has a room upstairs after all.

As you can imagine, at this point, I needed to have a look at that box. There was a strange-looking padlock through the handles on the front of it and it was sealed tight with this thick black wax all around the edges, so I didn't think the Count had to worry about anybody opening it, even if they wanted to. I shook it gently, and it was quite light like it was almost empty. But, just in case, I held it to my ear for a moment, listening. I thought maybe it might be a bomb, you know, especially after what happened with that Unabomber guy down in the States recently.

Well, there wasn't any ticking, but after a couple of seconds, I could have sworn I heard something go 'tap-tap-tap'. I know I'm not crazy, but it sounded like something was knocking from inside and wanting to be let out. I put the box down pretty quick and stuck it in a lower cabinet out of sight. I never wanted to touch it again but knew that I had to for the money the Count gave me. Not to mention that if I didn't follow through this 'friend' of his might get pissed off and cause a scene and get me fired on New Year's Eve."

"Thank you, Mr. O'Malley."

***

With a click, John turned off the tape recorder. After three-quarters of an hour of negotiating winding frost-filled curves, he pulled his unmarked Suburban to a stop under the resort's covered entrance, stopping directly behind Jansen's still idling Ford.

Harder stepped from his large Chevy, his breath surrounding him in a cloud of vapour as he exhaled the warmer air from inside the vehicle. It was bitterly cold up here on the Hill this morning. Before he'd left home, the thermometer hanging on the nail in his carport had said it was twenty-five below outside. He knew from experience that meant that it had to be at least minus thirty-five up here on the mountain top.

He approached the blue and white Crown Victoria idling in front of the main doors. Apart from a security sweep of the hotel perimeter every hour or so, he'd mandated that Jansen keep watch outside the hotel only. She had told John she was more than okay with that and would not enter the Sinclair until he returned. Harder didn't want any more of his members getting swallowed by the resort like Eggelson. He was concerned that Jansen felt some of what happened to the constable was her fault, which wasn't true, and didn't want her searching the building for him on her own in the middle of the night.

Exhaust coiled upward in a thick cloud into the frigid air, obscuring the cruiser for a moment. John reached into the cloud of vapour and rapped on the frosted driver's side window a couple of times. He expected Jansen to roll it down, but it remained closed. He rapped again, figuring perhaps she was napping and didn't hear him. The door was unlocked, and he pulled it open, meaning to reprimand the young officer. The interior dome light was on, but the cruiser was empty. He'd left explicit instructions for Jansen not to enter the building under any circumstance, and yet she had apparently done so, disobeying his direct order. Not good, he thought, not good.

Taking two long strides to the top of the steps, he thrust the main doors open. Jansen was nowhere in sight. He hadn't seen her portable radio in the cruiser, and he hoped that meant she had it on her person. Grabbing his shoulder mic, he tried to bring her up on the radio, but there was no response after several attempts. Depending on the structure they were inside, these radios could sometimes be practically useless. Fortunately, the Sinclair was not one of those buildings, and the reception had been acceptable in most areas, despite all the stone and concrete. But some sections, such as near the ballroom and the royal suite, were a dead zone for all radio transmissions.

Corporal Jansen wasn't answering her radio for only one of two reasons, and they were both bad. He hoped to God he was wrong, but either way, he found himself praying for the first time ever in his career that a co-worker had fallen ill or become incapacitated in some way. Because if she wasn't, then the only other possibility was something far, far worse.

CHAPTER FIFTEEN

December 24th, 2021 0759 hours

Overtop two ornate doors, a bronze-lettered banner sign read, 'Movie Theatre, Swimming Pool & Games Room Access'. Across from them, two more elegant doors led off to a different wing, labelled, 'Banquet & Ballroom Facilities'. A large, white plastic sign with red lettering was screwed into the decorative surface of the right-hand door beneath, covering most of it. Looking over Lively's shoulder, Minerva read it aloud, "'No Admittance, Authorised Personnel Only!' Oh my, what shall we do now? Is this a job, perhaps, for another one of your little friends?"

Lively stared at the two brilliant brass doorknobs before him for a long moment, then said, "Yes, it is, actually, because I remember this trick from last night." He reached for his pair of leather gloves, stuffed into a single pocket in his bomber jacket.

Minerva left Lively to figure out which of his gloves would contain which thumb and moved around him. She grasped the right door's handle and turned it gently, clicking the pair open. Her hand on the edge of the door handle, she turned back to Lively and said, "I guess we're authorised."

"Sis! Be careful with your hands around here. You can get frostbite from almost anything. Keep your gloves on. I tried turning the front door handle last night, and it was more than tongue-sticking to the flagpole cold. I swear I almost took off some skin." He flashed his palm at Minerva, displaying slightly reddened skin.

Minerva held up her smooth, ungloved hand and smiled sweetly. "See? Nothing! I'm okay. And the front door handle was fine when I arrived. It was cold, but only because it's almost thirty below outside."

"Well, when I touched it, it was like it had been in the vacuum of space. So, I guess I'm just saying be careful." He gestured Minerva inside, tilting his head slightly as he did, saying, "Ladies first."

"Thank you, but you know I'm a liberated woman. And besides, it's supposed to be age before beauty, Big Brother," Minerva stayed where she was and held her arm out to show him the way, instead.

Lively smiled and nodded, deferring to her advice. "I'm only older by two minutes, remember."

"Well, you certainly don't look it."

"Gee, thanks."

Cloudy overhead globes lining the lengthy corridor bathed everything in a sickly hue. The paisley-patterned carpet beneath their feet looked muted, coated like everything else in the hotel with a thick layer of dust that had collected over the years.

"It doesn't seem like this renewal, or whatever you want to call it, has stretched to this part of the hotel, yet," Minerva observed. She tapped one of her toes on the dusty carpet for emphasis, stirring up a small cloud of dust.

"I noticed that."

"Maybe it just takes a little longer. Sort of working its way from the inside out?"

"Perhaps," Lively replied, his gaze fixed on the corridor's wall. The wallpaper, having the advantage of its vertical orientation, was relatively dust-free compared to the carpeting. The paper had an engaging style that Lively knew he just had to stop and inspect. Colourful red and green foil leaves and vines were layered over top of each other, intertwining amongst themselves in various patterns. As he looked closer, it became apparent that some of the vines weren't actually vines after all, but something else entirely. "My, this is amazingly unpleasant." He made a sour expression.

Minerva moved next to him and scrutinised the wallpaper as well. Hidden fauna blended tastefully and unobtrusively with the flora in the paper's pattern. Twisted in amongst the colourful foliage were dozens of snakes, coiling and writhing, their mouths open and fangs piercing outward. To the casual eye, it was not readily apparent. But to those that chose to peer more closely at the world around them, it stood out quite clearly. Wrinkling her nose in distaste, Minerva said, "Who picked this paper out? Medusa?"

"I was thinking maybe Snake Pliskin," Lively suggested.

"Snake who?"

"Pliskin!"

With a small sigh, Minerva asked, "Which one is it this time?"

"It's 'Escape From New York', of course. It's a classic! You know... Kurt Russell? Donald Pleasence? With Adrienne Barbeau? Directed by her husband, John Carpenter?"

"Of course," Minerva nodded.

"Can't beat the classics, Sis," Lively said over his shoulder, moving down the corridor.

"Maybe with a big enough stick, you can," Minerva retorted with a smile. Her three and a half-inch boot heels clicked mutedly on the dust-thickened carpet as she trailed behind Lively. They passed entrances to two other ballrooms along the way without a second glance. "How do you know it's the last one?"

"I think it's pretty obvious," Lively replied, looking further along the corridor. At its end, a set of dual doors sported a thick chain running through both handles with a heavy, hardened brass padlock in the centre securing them. Stretching across the doorway, as if for good measure, a spiderweb of yellow police tape proclaimed, 'Police Line, Do Not Cross!'

Minerva said, "Well, okay, apart from that obvious clue." As they moved closer, she added, "Wow, was that meant to keep someone out, or something in?"

"Maybe a little of both," Lively said, lifting the heavy padlock to examine it. He hoped half-heartedly the key might still be in it but shook his head when he saw that his optimism had not proven prophetic. "Uh-oh, it looks like we're locked out."

"And of course, it's the one time I forgot to bring my bolt cutters," Minerva said, shaking her head in mock-disappointment.

"You would think this would be a problem, wouldn't you?" Lively asked.

"I would, and I do," Minerva said, nodding. "Since I'm hardly able to unscrew a jar of gherkins at home, I don't think I can do much to help here. And I think it's highly unlikely that you can tear this chain in two or break the lock off with your bare hands. So, what now?"

"This is all too true. But fortunately, I brought along another little friend," Lively said, reaching toward his belt.

Noting the direction of Lively's hands, Minerva asked, "Oh, no, another friend? Is this the one I need to cover my eyes for?"

"Only if you're afraid of progress," Lively replied. With great care and deliberation (for Lively, there was no other way), he slowly removed his answer to their dilemma from a black leather pouch attached to his belt — it looked like a glue gun.

"Are we going to do some crafting now?" Minerva enquired brightly.

"Yes, I'm going to craft us an open door." Holding up the device in front of Minerva's face, Lively said, "Sis, I'd like you to meet my little friend, the Snap Gun."

"Nice to meet you, Mr. Gun," Minerva said, nodding solemnly toward the device.

"Do not mock the Snap Gun."

"I wasn't! I was only being polite. Now make it snappy!" Minerva flashed him a broad smile.

Lively grinned in amusement for a moment, then his expression became serious. He attached a thin steel rod to the end of the gun and inserted it into the lock's key path. Next, he took a metal tension wrench from the pouch and also stuffed it into the lock, twisting as he did. After several quick snaps of the gun's trigger, with a metallic clunk, the heavy brass lock suddenly dropped open and Lively said, "Et, voila!"

"Very impressive." Minerva clapped her hands softly together. "With skills like that, you could get on full time with the Canadian Automobile Association."

Lively twisted the lock and let it drop to the floor with a resounding thud. "I agree. And it's so much faster than my old-fashioned manual lockpicks."

"Your little friend has a very appropriate name." Minerva observed with a smile.

"Because of the noise it makes?"

"No, because it makes breaking and entering a snap, silly."

"I should have seen that coming," Lively said as he began removing strand after strand of the yellow police web from the doorframe. Disturbing years of accumulated dust and cobwebs, he sneezed while he worked.

"Bless your little heart!" Minerva said.

"Thanks," Lively said with a sniff. His voice straining from anticipation, he slowly reached for the door handle, saying, "What do we have behind door number one, Monty." The handle turned freely, and the dual oak doors creaked open a small crack, revealing only blackness.

Standing next to Lively, Minerva said in a hushed voice, "Let the games begin." She grasped the other knob and began pulling the left side door slowly open, with Lively following suit on the right.

He could hardly contain his excitement, his childhood fantasies finally coming true as the heavy doors squealed open in front of him. An immense, dark, and quiet room was revealed beyond. Being careful not to step across the threshold, he felt as if there were a yawning abyss before his feet. Lively pulled out his mini-LED flashlight and shone it around the inside of the darkened room.

"Good idea," Minerva said. Reaching into her small, royal purple backpack purse, she pulled out her own torch and clicked it on. The shaft of light sliced through the blackness to the other side of the vast room like a brilliant lighthouse beacon on a dark and stormy night.

"Good lord! What are you packing in that thing, a lightsabre?"

"Yes, young padawan," Minerva said, looking over at her brother with a slight smile. She then gave a very good impression of a particular, green-skinned alien, adding, "Use the light side, I do!"

Lively and Minerva shone their lights into the room, neither daring to step through the open doorway for a moment. They looked into the darkness in silence, giving the room a moment of peace, allowing it to slowly waken, and be reintroduced to the world after its four-decade nap.

Their beams picked out dozens of chairs set around tables, with cutlery and glasses still spread across their surface. A long banner on the other side of the room had come loose and drooped down at the far end, now only reading 'HAPPY NEW'. Light from the outside world was kept at bay by heavy, red velvet draperies pulled tightly closed.

"Can you feel that, Lively?" Minerva asked quietly, the usual musical hint of mirth no longer present in her voice. The temperature in the Grand Ballroom of the Sinclair Hotel Resort was frigid, and she could see her breath spiralling up into the darkness that lay outside of her flashlight's beam.

"Yeah, Sis, I can." Lively felt his own voice grow to a whisper, vapour poured from his mouth as if exhaling a cigar. He shone his light along the wall to his right and spotted a row of light switches. Running the edge of his hand along the bottom of the switches, he went down the row, flipping them up into the on position four at a time, and the darkened room sprung to light. They stood in the doorway and marvelled, their mouths agape, silenced by the sight that lay before them.

The room seemed to stretch into the distance due to its size, but it had to be an optical illusion, Then he recalled what Minerva had told him of her lobby adventure and wondered if perhaps there was a slight LIMEE at play in this room as well. Overhead, hammered copper ceiling tiles glowed warmly in the reflected light of dozens of dusty crystal chandeliers that hung row upon row from one end of the room to the other.

"My God," Minerva said. "This is nuts. It looks bigger than the Empress Ballroom in Blackpool!"

"I know. And that ballroom is over twenty-thousand square feet. But this has to be almost thirty-thousand."

"You're the one that said you wanted to go big or go home, remember?" Minerva asked.

"This is true. Well, let's see what we shall see." Putting his flashlight back into his jacket pocket, Lively rubbed his hands together with glee, looking for all the world like a little kid at Christmas. He slowly walked into the room, an expression of awe on his face. Just being here after so many years of wondering was, for him at least, a very powerful thing. He removed a Canon Digital SLR from his courier bag and draped the attached strap over his head, then began walking about the large room snapping picture after picture in a series of short burst shots. Seemingly satisfied, he let the Canon hang from its strap and proceeded to pull an ancient Polaroid Instant Land Camera from his bag's depths.

"Where on earth did you get that?" Minerva asked, looking at the Polaroid.

"Off the internet, just like everything else these days. Turns out you can buy them refurbished, and they even have third parties making film packs for them again." He lined up Minerva in the viewfinder and snapped a shot of her. The camera flash went off, and with a mechanical whirring noise, it spit out its print, and Lively handed it to her. With another flash and a whir, he took another picture of her and moved toward the bar.

Blinking from the flash, Minerva asked, "Why do you use a digital as well as an analogue camera?"

"Well, you never know what you'll pick up on film, I like to cover both bases, analogue and digital. Over the years, I've seen examples of both formats displaying paranormal phenomena."

"Fair enough," Minerva said, looking at the still-developing print for a moment. Inside the white-framed border, her face began to resolve out of the grey nothingness currently there. Her body developed next, followed by the background. She began to place the print in her pocket when she did a sudden double-take and said, "Oh, my."

"Minerva, what is it?" Lively asked, concerned, moving back toward his sister.

"You were right."

"About what?"

"Your film. I think it worked." She handed the print to Lively as he arrived.

Dotted about the room in the picture's background, dozens of orbs of light floated in the air, faintly, but clearly visible, as if someone had inflated transparent balloons and placed them behind Minerva. "Wow! I mean, holy crap!"

"What?"

"It looks like they're all still here! Those faint light orbs all around you. I think it's them."

"The missing people? Are you sure it isn't an issue with the lens?"

"Well, there is a photographic term called 'backscatter' which explains the light orbs away as being things such as dust, insects, pollen, etcetera. But there are many people out there who say otherwise and believe that they are the souls of departed individuals."

"So, you think they're all dead?"

"I'm not saying that. I don't know. And that's why we're here. But at least this is something to start on. We're going to need to do a reading here this evening." Lively handed the print back to his sister.

"I agree." Minerva placed the print in her pocket and pulled a microcassette audio recorder from her small backpack. "Look at this, it's even analogue old school, just like you."

"Nice! There is no school like the old school. So, are you going to make some notes about this?"

"No, I'm going to try recording some EVP. You know, Electronic Voice Phenomena? Like you said, you never know what you're going to pick up."

"That's a great idea!" Lively pulled out an elongated piece of grey plastic from his courier bag. It had an analogue needle readout on the front and a row of coloured lights running from green to red along the top, currently unilluminated. "I brought my EMF reader with me as well. You never know when an unexpected field of electromagnetic radiation might pop out of nowhere and need to be measured."

Minerva nodded, saying, "Fabulous! And if we want, later, we can go around checking all the old Amana microwaves in the suites for leaks."

Lively smiled slightly. That girl seemed to have a comeback for everything he said, and he loved her for it. He began snapping more shots about the room with his cameras. Every time he took a Polaroid, he would shake the picture back and forth for several seconds, holding it with the tips of his fingers, then place it in his jacket pocket to finish developing. With that done, he would alternate to the digital SLR hanging around his neck and take a few more shots with that. His EMF reader came next. After a quick scan, he would switch back to the Land camera, then rinse and repeat.

Leaving Lively to his photographic endeavours, Minerva explored the room, holding her recorder out in front of herself. Every once in a while, she would stop and ask one of several questions. "Are there any spirits here that wish to communicate? We mean you no harm and only want to help. Speak to us, spirits." She would then stop the recorder and play it back, checking if she'd received any response to her queries.

The bandstand was in the far corner of the room. A grand piano sat nearby with its bench pulled out just a little bit. It was perfectly positioned, looking as if someone were still sitting there, playing silently and invisibly, decade after decade, inside this darkened room. Minerva approached it, making her recordings as she went. She stood at one end of the piano and tinkled the keys slightly, noting the discordant sound they made. After so many years of sitting, it was now badly out of tune.

Minerva asked another question, "Will you play me some memories?" After ten seconds or so, she stopped recording, rewound the tape and played it back. Her melodic voice repeated her recent question, followed by a faint hiss of dead air. She was getting ready to press stop when an almost imperceptible but audible tinkle of piano keys came from the recorder's small speaker. It was as if someone had been sitting there all along, then, at the last moment, playfully plinked away at the topmost keys for her just a few times to tease her.

"My God, I think it worked!"

"What worked?"

"I picked up a faint sound of music on here."

"Are you using an old tape? Maybe that was already on there?"

"No, it's brand new."

"Make sure you keep that safe, then."

"Already on top of things, thanks." Moving toward the centre of the room, Minerva clicked a button on her recorder, marking the spot on her tape to ensure she didn't record over it by mistake in the future.

Near the room's middle, the hardwood floor was bare of tables and chairs, and Minerva found herself in the dance area. Something in the very middle of all this emptiness caught her attention; various shades of red, green, and gold all coiled together in a heap on the dusty hardwood floor. As she got closer to the mound, she sighed, relieved. Hundreds of balloons lay deflated and wrinkled amongst the streamers and confetti, like shed skin from dozens and dozens of colourful snakes. "Thank goodness. If it had been snakes, I'd have been out of here."

"What was that?" Lively called out from the other side of the room.

"Balloons and streamers. The floor here in the middle of the room is covered with them." She looked to the ceiling and saw some fine netting that must have contained them at one time.

Lively snapped and flashed his way across the room. Neither he nor Minerva disturbed the pile of derelict decorations, but instead stood at their edge, only marvelling at them.

"Moving anything in here feels like it would be the same as desecrating an ancient burial site," Lively commented.

"I agree," Minerva said, shuddering slightly.

"Look at how they form an almost perfect circle," Lively observed. "If people had danced through them, they would have been scattered all over the place, but that obviously didn't happen."

"So, at midnight, a timer must have tripped, and then this confetti of happiness dropped from the ceiling onto..."

"No one," Lively finished her thought. "It's like between the time of the clock hitting midnight and the blackout, everyone in here would have to have been gone already. I would say that as soon as the power went out, they disappeared in a matter of a split second, not fifteen seconds like everybody believes."

"But how is that even possible?" Minerva asked. "After all, we have verified witness reports stating that there were people inside this room minutes, sorry, seconds before the power went out."

Lively stood lost in thought, his chin resting in a cradle formed by his left hand, elbow resting on his crossed right forearm. "I think we need to step back and look at this from a bigger viewpoint," he said, nodding at the mound. "There's something that we're not seeing, we're just too close to the event."

"I agree. We need to look back to what happened at the hotel before the event."

"Over the years leading up to the mass disappearance, there were many reported cases of strange things happening here."

"I don't remember hearing about very many other things happening here, why is that?

"That's because they weren't very well reported. That is to say, Edward Sinclair apparently had deep enough pockets to not have anything appear in the media that he didn't want to appear." Lively reached into his ever-present courier bag and pulled an inch-thick bundle of paper that looked to be a book manuscript. "But luckily, good fortune has smiled upon us."

"And me without a lottery ticket."

He handed the document to Minerva, adding, "Don't worry, you're still a winner around here with one of these in your hands, Sis."

"My, aren't you the industrious one," Minerva said. She smiled at the artwork on the mock cover Lively had created — an iconic green spirit from a certain movie franchise sat behind a large circle with a red slash through the middle. The text below the infamous spook read, 'Big Book of Ballroom Busting.' She knew she shouldn't have expected anything less from her brother, who, thanks to the dozen years he'd spent with CSIS, had turned what was already an organised personality into one that was now almost obsessive-compulsive in its level of attention to detail. The fact that he'd basically written a book already said a lot of his devotion to the subject of the Sinclair mystery.

"I've taken the liberty of compiling all of the previously documented occurrences into one, easy-to-read-while-you-investigate bundle. It's got almost everything we know about the Sinclair Incident in one place. Hopefully, it will help us get our minds around this thing a bit better."

Minerva hefted the document, surprised by the weight. "Can I borrow it for a while? It looks like I've got my homework cut out for me."

Lively pulled out another copy of the manuscript from his bag and flashed it at her, saying, "That's okay, I have another copy. And don't worry, there're lots of pictures inside," Lively concluded with a mischievous grin.

With a smirk on her own face, Minerva swatted him on the shoulder with her now rolled-up manuscript. "Oh, you're a funny one, you are!"

"Always." Lively flashed a quick smile. He continued, "But seriously, I think it would be best if we split up."

Minerva made a shocked expression. "Oh, this is serious! I never saw the warning signs we were in any trouble." She shook her head in disbelief. "Who gets custody of the spirits?"

It was now Lively's turn to swat Minerva with his copy of the manuscript. "You're as bad as I am."

"No, I am two minutes less bad than you are, Big Brother. But yes, Mr. Serious, I agree. Isn't splitting up what everyone does in spooky old buildings?"

With a small smile, Lively said, "Yes, it is. That way, we can cover more ground and get into more trouble. I'll start in the basement, you take the third floor, and we'll work our way back toward each other. Oh, just so you know, I've also taken the liberty of breaking down the document into sections."

Minerva flipped the manuscript open and leafed through dozens of plastic tabs along the right side, seeing such labels as Third Floor, Second Floor, Main Floor, Entertainment, Recreation, Basement'. In the 'Third Floor' section of the document, he had further broken it down with sub-tabs to indicate which wing of the floor the incident had occurred. "My, but you've been a busy little bee. When do you find the time?"

"Sometimes, I don't sleep very much."

"I can believe that."

"All right," Lively said, clapping his hands together, "I think I'm going to finish giving this room a quick once-over and then go exploring." He paused, then added, "Oh yeah! One more thing!"

Minerva had just started flipping through the 'manual' and paused, looking at Lively over the edge of the manuscript. "Yes?"

"Did you do the math yet?"

"Which math is that?"

"Well, this hotel opened on December 31st, 1946. The disappearance happened on December 31st, 1981."

"Technically, since it was midnight, it was 1982," Minerva added.

"Correct. So, what kind of math should you do with those numbers?"

"Well, if I add it up, it comes out to a total of seventy-four. Is there a pattern here that I'm missing?"

"Yes."

"Okay, are you going to tell me, or do I have to get my calculator out?"

Clearing his throat, Lively said in a teacherly voice, "I'll give you a little hint. Prime numbers."

Minerva looked at him blankly for a moment, then said, "Okay, from when the resort opened until the incident occurred was thirty-seven years, which is a prime number."

"Correct again. But remember, there are other prime numbers between two and thirty-seven you know."

"Thanks, I am aware of that fact," Minerva said, but sported a slightly puzzled expression, not looking quite sure she understood what Lively was getting at.

"Things happened on other dates around here as well," Lively said, tapping the manuscript. "Did you know, if you add the forty-six from the year this place opened to the prime numbers seventeen and nineteen, you'd get the date of the disappearance in 1982?"

Still looking perplexed, Minerva said, "I didn't know that. But why would you want to do that and break it up like that?"

"Because if you add seventeen to forty-six that would take us to December 1963. Then, if you add the nineteen onto it, you get to 1982."

"December 1963? Okay, so now things add up to a Four Seasons song title. And?"

"Oh, there's much more to it than that."

"Okay, I give, what happened in December of 1963 that I should be aware of?"

Lively was having fun, dancing around his denouement, but took pity on Minerva and said, "Why, the death and disappearance on Christmas Eve 1963, of course. Personally, just between you and me, I think it may have been a murder-suicide."

"Murder-suicide? I never remember hearing about that. Do we have Edward Sinclair's deep pockets to thank for covering up that as well?"

Lively tapped Minerva's manuscript lying on the table once more, saying only, "Read on, Macduff," then moved toward the entrance of the ballroom.

With a slight shake of her head and a small smile, Minerva pulled out a chair from one of the dusty tables. She reached into her purple pack and dug around. After a moment, she pulled out a camel hair bristle brush and began dusting off the seat of the chair as well as a spot on the table. Only then did she sit down and crack the spine of the manuscript.

Lively watched this operation from the ballroom entrance and smiled, feeling an overwhelming sense of brotherly love for his sister. Despite her protestations otherwise, she had almost as many personality quirks as he had.

He headed back toward the basement, not needing to refresh his memory of the events of that snowy evening as they were burned into his brain. December 24th, 1963 was the date of the very first major 'incident' at the Sinclair Resort Hotel, and tonight was its anniversary.

CHAPTER SIXTEEN

December 24th, 1963 1900 hours

Signifying the hour to those unable to see it, the grandfather clock in the lobby rang seven long, sonorous tones. Vincent DaCosta was one of those people able to see the large clock, and he sighed, leaning resignedly on the ornately carved front desk. He was only one hour into his twelve-hour shift, and he was already bored out of his skull. Across the lobby, the minute hand crawled toward each roman numeral on the clock face. It was going to be another long, boring Christmas Eve. In the office at his back, sat a small black and white TV. From its single, tinny speaker emanated the first lilting strains of the song, Buffalo Gals, as the local TV station down in Entwistle began to play a static-filled broadcast of Frank Capra's classic, It's a Wonderful Life.

Across the lobby, the bartender at the Snowdrop Lounge, Tommy Dorfman, looked back at him with a similarly bored expression. It had been so quiet over at the lounge for Tommy this evening, he'd let the barmaid go home early. Rita something-or-other — Vincent couldn't keep track of the staff; they went through the people so quickly around this place. Sometimes, he'd just get to know someone's name, and they'd be gone the next day like they'd never existed.

Dorfman mimed loading bullets into an invisible gun now held in one hand. He cocked the trigger and put it to his temple. After a brief, imploring look toward Vincent, he pulled the imaginary trigger and collapsed behind the bar.

DaCosta just shook his head at Dorfman's shenanigans, as usual. He tracked his attention toward the sole occupants of the Snowdrop Lounge.

To one side of the entrance sat a group of a half-dozen, sombre-looking businessmen, all dressed in black. They were quite pale and gaunt with faces that looked like they might break if they attempted anything approaching a smile. According to Tommy, these businessmen, which he was currently ignoring, had arrived around four o'clock in the afternoon and claimed a corner table in the lounge near the entrance. The whole group had been strangely silent, not speaking a word, whether by choice or a language barrier no one was quite sure. There was one who spoke some English, and he ordered a bottle of vodka to share between them. However, they'd ordered no food or appetisers all evening and only sat sipping the vodka, neat.

Turning away from the group of men, Vincent eyed the key rack at his back. He noted how few rooms were rented this evening. With a sigh, he pushed back a lock of oily, dark hair from his forehead, then adjusted the thick-lensed eyeglasses on his nose, returning to the office to catch some of the movie that had recently started.

The last couple of Christmas Eves at the Sinclair, Vincent had the misfortune of having been assigned to work the front desk, just like tonight. But now that he knew what to expect, he planned accordingly. This evening, he'd brought along a thermos loaded with his 'Finest' holiday coffee to help pass the time. Mixed in with the java, cream and sugar were several healthy splashes of Ballantine's Finest Scotch Whiskey. Despite not being with family and friends tonight, at least he knew he could get comfortably numb. Hopefully, it would make some of the holiday drivel on the TV a little more entertaining.

With a smile and a flourish, Vincent poured the evening's first fistful of festive coffee into the twist-off cup that the thermos provided. He took a slow, savouring sip as he settled into a thickly padded office chair. The whiskey was already doing its job and burning its way down his throat. On the desktop TV, a young George Bailey was diving into icy waters to rescue his little brother, Harry. Vincent inhaled the vapour swirling up from his coffee and sighed complacently while he watched the drama unfold onscreen. It looked like George was going to save Harry again, just like last year, and the year before.

Brown penny-loafers sitting on the floor beneath his chair, Vincent made a small groan of pleasure as he stretched his legs out and rested his stocking feet on a second office chair facing toward him. This was so comfortable; he'd have to be careful he didn't fall asleep.

The front desk bell made three sharp dings. "Of course," he muttered. "Never fails." He begrudgingly stood upright, slipped his shoes back on and exited the office. Across the lobby from the front desk, a mirrored wall surrounded the lounge entrance, making the interior of the Sinclair appear quite a bit larger than it already was. With the angle he'd been sitting at, he should have been able to see any waiting customers reflected in this mirror, but tonight he hadn't seen anyone, which was very strange.

DaCosta stepped from the office alcove and saw that there was indeed a customer waiting to be served, an extremely tall and dangerously thin gentleman. He was well dressed in a deep-black pinstripe suit that definitely hadn't come off the rack at Woodward's Department Store. Atop his head, a bowler hat was perched at a jaunty angle. The man just stood there, not saying anything, studying Vincent, a twinkle of amusement in his eyes.

Vincent looked at the man, confused. If this man had come from the upper floors of the hotel, he should have seen him. When drinking his Christmas Cheer, DaCosta liked to have a clear view of the elevator and stairs from his seat in the semi-darkened office, just in case someone wandered up to the front desk, such as right now.

"Good evening sir, welcome to the Sinclair. How may I assist you?" As he spoke, he wondered how this man had entered the hotel without him hearing the front doors open and close — the TV wasn't up that loud. And he wasn't part of the sombre-looking group of gentlemen from across the lobby, since all six men still sat there, staring blankly at their drinks. His confusion mounted as he took in the man's clothing. Why wasn't he covered in snow? It was falling fast and thick outside the office window. How did this guy get up the mountain in the first place? His ride would have had to pull right past the office window where Vincent sat, and there had been no vehicle. Plus, even someone stepping from their car under the covered entrance would still have had a bit of snow on their person. But this man did not have a speck of snow on him, nor was he wearing an overcoat, just a regular business suit despite the sub-zero weather.

In a low, grave voice, Mr. Bowler Hat said, "Starting your Nativity celebrations early this evening, my friend?"

"I'm sorry?" Vincent said, unsure of what the man meant, but suspecting it was the obvious thing.

The man in the hat continued, "I have a very sensitive nose, young man, and right now, I can smell the distinctive aroma of some very fine Scotch Whiskey — Ballantine's, I believe it is, and it's coming from you." The man pointed one long, rather bony finger in Vincent's general direction.

"That's an excellent nose you've got, sir. But it's just a little something to take the chill off — with the time of year being taken into account and all," he said apologetically. Vincent really didn't want to get in trouble for drinking on the job on Christmas Eve.

But he need not have worried, as the man said, "Far be it for me to suggest anything otherwise, my fine fellow! I'm all-in for a man having a bracer or two and enjoying himself on Christmas Eve! And I'm quite sure it's brightened your evening already, hasn't it?" the man inquired with a crooked, toothy smile.

Under the recessed lights of the front desk, a large diamond stickpin sparkled in the centre of Bowler Hat's crisply knotted, red silk tie, dazzling Vincent with its brilliance. Averting his gaze slightly, he asked, "What can I do for you, sir?"

"Oh, it's not what you can do for me, it's what I can do for you!" the thin man exclaimed grandly.

"I'm sorry, sir, I don't know what you mean." Vincent figured maybe this guy had already been in his own cups tonight — or perhaps it was because his mental elevator didn't quite make it up to the penthouse. Either way, he was an odd duck.

"It appears that things are rather slow this evening, is that correct, Vincent?" The man watched DaCosta's eyes widen slightly, then added, "I am so sorry, may I call you Vincent?"

Feeling taken aback, DaCosta looked down at his chest and realised he didn't have his name tag pinned to his shirt. He must have forgotten. "Of course not, sir, but h-how did you know my first name?"

"I saw it written on the register in front of you, of course, Vincent," Mr. Bowler Hat explained.

He looked down at the register. The man was not lying. He would have been able to see Vincent's name from where he stood, scribbled in under the section that read 'shift supervisor'. But the fact that this man could read it upside down and decipher Vincent's left-handed chicken scrawl simultaneously said something for the man's eyes. They were apparently as sharp as his nose. He wondered what else was sharp about this man. Glancing back up, he said, "Of course, sir. How can I help you?"

Bowler Hat replied, "As I said, I am here to do something for you," and after a pause, he added, "and to give something to you."

"And what would that be, sir?"

"Why, give you some business, of course!"

"The Sinclair is always open for business, sir."

"Yes, indeed it is." The man smiled crookedly. "However, I have a proposal for you, my young friend."

Okay, here it comes. What's this guy all about? The thin man looked vaguely familiar, but Vincent couldn't quite place where he'd seen his face. He steeled himself and asked, "And what would that be, sir?"

"Well, I have a half dozen business associates meeting me here this evening. They're from overseas, however, and don't speak any English. They would have arrived earlier this afternoon."

Vincent nodded and thought it strange that the man didn't seem to notice or chose to ignore the fact that the group of men he was referring to appeared to be sitting across the lobby from him, still sipping their glasses of vodka, neat. And Mr. Bowler Hat couldn't have failed to notice them sitting there if he'd entered the hotel from the outside. Strange, again.

– 138 –

Disrupting Vincent's line of thought, the man continued, "I have reserved the royal suite for the night to use as a conference room while my associates and I tend to our business. However, I have no doubt we'll all be feeling quite peckish just around midnight, and we would certainly appreciate a late-night bite delivered up to us at that time. Do you foresee any problem in accommodating this request, Vincent?"

DaCosta opened his mouth to tell the man that due to it being Christmas Eve, the kitchen closed early at 9:00 P.M. But then, Bowler Hat slid a hundred-dollar bill across the desk, and Vincent's jaw snapped shut with a crack. Reaching his right hand across the counter, Vincent discretely palmed the money, and said, "Absolutely not, sir! There won't be any problem at all with your requests!" He would have whatever this guy wanted for a snack left on ice for a few hours and then have it delivered at midnight. Problem solved.

"Fabulous!" The man clapped his hands together in apparent glee. "I will look forward to your service at midnight!" He produced a small off-white envelope from an inner pocket with a flourish and slid it across the desk toward DaCosta. On top of it, another hundred-dollar bill sat destined for Vincent's pants pocket. The man said, "Here is a list of delicacies for our midnight repast, please see that the kitchen follows these directions to the letter."

"Absolutely sir, no problem." He turned the desk register around to face the man, saying, "I will need you to fill your name and address here in the book, please."

"Of course!" Bowler hat took the ballpoint pen from the imitation inkwell on the desk and scribbled away for a moment in the register.

While this happened, Vincent turned to consult the reservation book that sat on the counter beneath the key rack. He wanted to verify that the man was indeed booked in like he said. The reservation must have come through sometime during the day today when he was off duty. He'd neglected to look at the reservation book since starting his shift, and he did so now, opening it and flipping to the current day. Sure enough, there was a name filled in the reservation book for the royal suite. He took the key from the top pigeonhole of the rack then turned back to the man. As he handed the key to Bowler hat, the man said, "Oh, one other thing, Vincent. Could you please ensure that you deliver our midnight buffet yourself?"

"Absolutely, sir!" DaCosta said with a broad smile. "I'll be there at the stroke of twelve with your food."

"Splendid! We'll look forward to your joining us at midnight then!" He crossed the lobby toward the elevator and pressed the call button when he arrived. The car began to descend from the third floor, and Bowler Hat turned and clapped his hands together loudly several times as if trying to catch the attention of some errant dogs or small children.

At the sound of the handclapping, Vincent watched the vodka drinking businessmen rise as one and depart the lounge. They filed silently toward the elevator in a single line. When the door opened with a ping, still wholly ignoring the group of men, Bowler Hat stepped aside, let the group file inside, and then walked on board last. As the elevator doors slid shut, the man turned and faced outward, gazing toward the front desk. He looked directly into Vincent DaCosta's eyes and gave another broad, toothy smile.

A chill slowly rolled its way up DaCosta's spine, ending at his shoulder blades, which spasmed uncontrollably together for a moment. When he'd looked at the reservations book, he'd only verified there was a name and hadn't double-checked what it was, until now. Stuffing the crumpled money into his pants pocket, Vincent turned the register back around to see what name the man had used, and his breath caught in his throat.

'Max Schreck' had been written in the book with a flourish like the man had been writing it for years. However, that couldn't be the man's real name, Vincent thought, shaking his head in confusion. And yet, for some reason, he felt sure the name the man had used was, in fact, correct. While he realised that another man could share this same name, there was a problem with that. Apart from Bowler Hat's diamond stickpin and dated hat, the most striking thing about him had been his mouthful of distinctive, misshapen teeth.

Growing up, one of Vincent's favourite movies, and one which still creeped him out to this very day, had been 'Nosferatu'. In addition to a bald head and fingernails like Fu Manchu, the actor in that film had sported a gobful of dreadful dentistry, making it a focal point of the iconic makeup he wore in his portrayal of ancient Transylvanian evil.

Vincent would have sworn on a stack of bibles that the man here tonight and the actor Max Schreck were, in fact, one and the same. But that brought him back to his problem. First of all, Schreck, the actor, would be over one hundred years old now, and not in his fifties as Bowler Hat appeared to be. And then there was the other small problem: film actor Max Schreck had died of a heart attack in 1936.

DaCosta knew the Sinclair Hotel was creepy at the best of times. But now that people who had been dead for a quarter-century were checking into the place, it felt even more so. Christmas Eve had just gotten interesting for him, but not quite in the way he'd anticipated.

CHAPTER SEVENTEEN

January 2nd, 1982 0755 hours

Harder scanned the lobby for any immediate sign of Corporal Jansen, but she was nowhere in sight. It felt cold in here now, and not just because one of the main doors still stood open at his back. Since all of the heating in this hotel was electric, and since the power was still on, it should have been a balmy seventy-two degrees in the lobby. He noted this new frigid atmosphere with concern; it seemed almost as extreme as what he'd encountered in the ballroom.

He moved to the middle of the lobby, his footfalls echoing off the polished marble floors and thick stone walls, sounding as if a small army of John Harders were following along behind him in pursuit. Trying the radio again, he said, "Corporal Jansen! Please respond!" but received only silence in response.

After waiting a beat, he strode toward the corridor leading to the ballrooms, then turned and called out in a thunderous baritone, "Corporal Jansen, report!"

John took in the lobby, listening intently as he did. His breath steamed around him in a cloud of vapour. Thanks to his sharp eyes, he had been a signalman in the Royal Canadian Navy during the war. A sudden flash of movement near the front desk caught his attention. For the briefest moment, he was sure he'd caught sight of someone standing at the top of the staircase, watching him from the shadows.

"Halt! RCMP!" Harder shouted. Unfortunately, this 'person of interest' chose to ignore John, turned, and fled down the basement stairs.

Now, John was angry, and he didn't like getting angry. Whoever they were, they weren't stopping, and he was going to have to give chase. Not a man easily stirred to movement, Harder was a sight to behold once he was in motion. His powerful legs pounded down the stairs two at a time. Halfway to the bottom of the staircase, it doglegged to the left. John hit the small landing at full speed and rebounded off the wall slightly from the force of his momentum. He corrected course and then flew down the final flight of stairs to the double service door.

John burst into the corridor, trying to look both directions at the same time. There was no one in sight. To his left, just across the hallway, a door latch was snicking shut. John lunged toward the doorknob and cranked it open, pushing through a door labelled 'Mechanical/Electrical/Pump Room'.

A maze of cables, pipes and wiring stood before him. This immediate area seemed to be the main mechanical room. No one was directly in view, but that was to be expected. The room branched off into several different directions, each seeming to serve one of the hotel's critical needs. Cables, conduits, and pipes crisscrossed the ceiling of the room. A series of switches, gauges, knobs and dials projected from one wall.

John called out, his deep voice resonating off of the numerous hard surfaces in the room, "This is Inspector John Harder of the Royal Canadian Mounted Police. You are trespassing in an open crime scene. Surrender yourself now!"

There was no response. John was forced to choose a direction, and he favoured his right, a long, damp corridor, sloping slightly downward lay before him. John did not draw his service revolver; instead, he extracted his heavy-duty flashlight from its holster on his belt. At the very least, he could use it on the suspect to disable him if he proved violent. John was not a fan of using any more force than necessary to subdue someone. And this someone, whoever they were, hadn't shown any indication of having a weapon. So, unless the individual had a knife, John knew he had the advantage.

The further along that John moved, the damper it became until he could almost feel the heavy moisture in the air beading on his skin. A cloying musty smell filled the corridor. At its end, a door labelled 'Pump Room' stood open halfway. He entered cautiously, scanning the room as he moved, but saw no immediate threat. Several man-sized, heavy-duty pumps lined one wall, their feeder pipes and outflows intertwining like snakes. He followed the pipes and was led down another shorter corridor toward a secondary room, its door standing ajar. John approached slowly, ready for anything.

In the centre of the room was a wellhead. It was capped by an immensely heavy-looking, domed, steel cap. The feeder pipes ended in this room, snaking down into the floor next to the well cap. A steady drip of condensation from overhead pipes dribbled rhythmically onto the grey concrete beneath, giving the floor a glossy sheen. It was very cold in here, and though John's breath wasn't quite steaming at the moment, he felt it was on the verge. Any colder, and this room would be a skating rink. He was glad of the well cap. Without it, he could imagine slipping on unseen ice, sliding across the floor, and then plummeting into the gaping, black throat of the well. It had been covered to keep people from accidentally falling into the well while servicing the pipes in this room.

Something lay next to the wellhead, shining starkly in the white light of the overhead fluorescents. It looked familiar. John knelt next to the well cap to examine the item, his knees popping. It was a cap badge from the hat of an RCMP police officer. With two members already missing, it could belong to either one of them. Sometimes, members had their officer numbers engraved on the back of their badges. John flipped it over and saw he was in luck, there was a number.

His heart stopped beating in his chest for a moment, and he double-checked the number — he had to because what he saw in front of him was impossible. It couldn't be there in his hand right now, but it was. A piece of cold, hard metal, with an officer number engraved into it which he would never forget. It was that of his late son, Danny. But how did it get here? His mind felt on overload and about to blow. This did not compute.

Thoroughly shaken, John placed the badge carefully in his pocket. The wound caused by his recent loss was still fresh in his heart. And seeing that cap badge here right now had felt like a knife had just been jammed into it again and twisted, hard.

A feeling of nausea threatened to overwhelm him, and he remained kneeling, and examined the steel cap over the wellhead instead.

Disappearances and accidents were almost the norm during the hotel's construction, as John had come to understand it. And much of that had been blamed on drugs and alcohol. Since the development of the resort had begun immediately after the Second World War, many of the construction workers had been soldiers returning home, looking for peace in their lives, and a steady job.

Unfortunately, Post Traumatic Stress Disorder was an issue for many of them. They'd simply called it shell shock when John had been in the service, but no matter which way you sliced it, it was still horrible what war could do to a man and how its after-effects could destroy their lives.

A large number of these returning soldiers dealt with their condition through drugs and alcohol, and there were several instances of men injuring themselves on the job due to inebriation. If a worker was discovered under the influence, they were usually fired immediately, but the problem was still rampant at the site.

Johnny Dillon had been the man in charge of the pump's final installation before it was turned on. He'd been left alone down in the well room at the end of the day, running through his final checklist, and testing all of the assorted nuts, bolts, and pipe fittings. And that was the last anyone had ever seen of him.

Many presumed Johnny was another broken man from the war who had drifted to another job in another town — just one more vet with a substance abuse problem that had flown the coop in the middle of the night and little had been thought of it.

The pump was turned on for the first time the next day without Johnny in attendance, or so they thought. Everything went swimmingly for the first little while, until the water pressure dropped.

Dillon's water-logged body had been found stuck in the pump's main intake pipe. After he'd been removed and everything cleaned up, the Sinclair had fresh, spring water flowing through its gleaming new pipes once more.

However, there was one small thing they neglected to mention — the water still contained a hint of Johnny Dillon, just a small piece that they couldn't locate when they retrieved his body.

And that had been his head. It had never been found despite several volunteers being lowered into the two-hundred-foot deep well to search for it afterwards.

Harder stood, feeling his knees pop a second time in complaint. He turned and moved toward the exit.

At his back, the faintest of noises.

Tap-tap-tap.

He paused and turned back to the well cap. After a moment, the sound came again, a little louder this time.

Tap-tap-tap.

It was coming from beneath the steel well cap, like somebody was on the other side, knocking to be let in, or out.

The cap had to weigh several hundred pounds. It would be almost impossible for one person to lift it by themselves to gain entry. Plus, it looked as if it were never meant to be opened again. The dome-like lid had been welded shut all the way around its circumference, including the hinges. He leaned down to look closer. The welds on the steel were old, not recent.

Tap-tap-tap.

The sound grew fainter and fainter, like the person's energy was running out. As if, after somehow climbing up all this way in the dark, grasping onto the slippery, slimy stones that lined the shaft and finally making it all the way to the top, they'd found the lid closed and were now only able to weakly tap at the cold steel instead.

There was just the faintest of taps now. Whoever, or whatever was on the other side, seemed to have given up. Maybe it was just pressure in the pipes, after all, John reasoned. Putting his ear within a couple of inches of the lid, he strained to hear anything more.

From the other side of the cap came a pounding blow. Harder was lifted off the lid by several inches from the concussive force, and he was neither a light nor a small man. His heart felt like it did a somersault in his chest, which was a rare thing. He was not an easily frightened man either, perhaps due to his size and training, and he had rarely experienced any real fear, not since WW2. That was, until now.

He sat on the cold concrete floor, leaning back on his palms, and looking at the steel lid in shock. Perspiration dripped from his forehead as his mind tried to think of a logical explanation for this, but it didn't come.

In a shaken voice, he asked, "Is anyone down there?" even though he knew for a fact that there couldn't be. According to the staff he'd questioned previously, it was a closed system at the bottom and did not extend to any other areas of the hotel. Instead, it connected to an aquifer far beneath the ground, extending eventually to the river beyond. There was no possible way anybody could have come in from anywhere else. So, whatever had crawled out of the bowels of the earth from below, and was now tapping behind the domed steel lid, was nothing human.

Nevertheless, he called out, "Is there anybody there?" He leaned forward on his haunches and knocked gently three times. He sat back and waited, not willing to put his face near the lid again.

"Who's on the other side of this lid? Are you trapped?" Harder moved a hair closer, but not by much. He waited for several moments. There was no further response from the other side of the lid, and he stood, legs feeling rather weak. A slight wave of dizziness washed over him, and he leaned for a moment near the doorway, one hand against the cold, damp concrete wall.

With a puff, Harder moved slowly back along the corridor on slightly rubbery legs. Arriving back in the pump room, the temperature felt like it had dropped further — the dampness on the floor was suddenly taking on an icy sheen. He reached out and ran his hands along the damp wall, feeling its frozen slickness. He'd have to be careful how he moved, or he might slip.

The main control room lay just ahead. Another few twists and turns and the hatchway to hell back there would be far behind him. And yet, part of him was still on duty, keeping an eye out for the suspect he'd been chasing earlier. He had a feeling he'd never know who or what it was that had led him down here on this chase. And what of Jansen and Eggelson? Were they still wandering the halls of this hotel? Was it one of them that he'd followed down here? Had they both suffered a mental slip from the stress of this situation and started stalking the halls of the Sinclair themselves in addition to whatever else dwelt here? His mind was on overload with these thoughts and more.

The overhead lights flared to supernova for a moment, causing John to shield his eyes from the glare – and then they went out completely.

He clicked on his flashlight, grasping it close to the head, its shaft resting along his shoulder. Holding it as he did allowed him to point it freely, and also enabled him to pivot his wrist if need be and use the heavy battery-filled shaft as a club to defend himself.

As he cast the light's beam rapidly about, it felt like a weapon in more ways than one. If the suspect came at him from out of the darkness, he was prepared to use it to subdue them with a flick of his wrist. But a part of him also hoped it could be used as a weapon against whatever insanity stalked the darkness down here.

With a sigh of relief, he saw the gauges and dials of the control room up ahead now — almost there.

At his back came a cracking sound as if old metallic bones were being broken.

What in the world was that? Was the building collapsing? And then he realised what it was, it was the welds cracking around the domed well cap — the ones that kept the ponderous piece of steel firmly shut.

John swept his light's beam back down the corridor but saw nothing. He spun back around and continued toward the control room and the exit.

As he moved, a new sound came from the well room. It was one he didn't want to hear or believed he would ever hear, the slow squeal of rusty metal on metal as the heavy lid over the well creaked open.

This isn't happening, John thought. I can't be hearing this — it's impossible! He continued sweeping his light, moving quickly but cautiously toward the exit.

With a crash, it sounded as if the lid had reached its tipping point and then smashed backwards onto the concrete floor — whatever had wanted to get out of the well was now free to join John inside the hotel.

Halfway across the control room, his flashlight began to flicker and fade. But the batteries were new! He'd replaced them just a couple of days prior. The light had seen minimal use since, so they should be almost full. John's knuckles whitened around the flashlight's head. He rattled the light to try and get it to brighten, hoping for a loose bulb or something. The flashlight briefly brightened, and he felt hopeful for a moment, but then it went out as well. There were no windows anywhere down here, and he was now completely blind in the darkness and had to stop.

"Shit!" He smacked the light against the open palm of his hand now to try and get it working, but to no avail.

From down the corridor leading to the pumps and well room, a new sound came to John — the wet slap of cold waterlogged flesh smacking onto the concrete floor as the thing from the other side of the well cap slowly approached his current position.

Harder moved as fast as he could through the control room, feeling along the wall with his left hand as he moved, his useless flashlight held out defensively in his right. He received some small comfort when his fingers finally traced over several banks of knobs and switches. He was nearing the exit, and moved rapidly now, hands probing out in front, searching for where he thought the door was located.

"Yes!" John whispered as his hand found the round, cold steel of the doorknob. He started turning it desperately back and forth, but it was locked. The tendons in his wrist felt like they were threatening to tear loose from the force he applied to the handle as he tried to turn the lock's tumblers past their breaking point, but it wouldn't budge.

Sweat beaded his brow, and he paused, listening intently into the silent blackness that surrounded him.

There was nothing now. No more wet flopping noises or the sound of anything waterlogged dripping slowly toward him. That was a good thing, John thought, maybe this horror show was finally over.

The musty, damp smell in his nostrils was suddenly replaced by something he liked even less: the smell of rotten meat. A heavy hand dropped onto his shoulder, and a thick, wet voice whispered in his ear, "Father."

CHAPTER EIGHTEEN

December 24th, 1963 2345 hours

Vincent DaCosta awoke with a snort. He felt disoriented. The last thing he remembered seeing was George Bailey's crestfallen face upon discovering he couldn't leave for college, because he needed to stay in Bedford Falls and run the family business after his father died of a heart attack. DaCosta shared George's pain, feeling unfulfilled in his own grand aspirations of fame and fortune. He knew it to be true, since here he was, manning the front desk of an isolated Canadian mountaintop resort in the middle of winter, on the graveyard shift, on Christmas Eve. There was no justice in the world, he thought sourly.

Currently on the TV across from his stocking feet, a spiritually energised Ebenezer Scrooge sat next to Mrs. Dilbert on the stairs, trying to convince her that he wasn't crazy. He suddenly ruffled his fingers through his thinning white hair at her, doing little to advance his case, and she screamed, ready to flee.

Checking the glowing radium dial of his wristwatch, Vincent was shocked to see the time was 11:47 P.M. He would need to take the midnight snack cart up to the freak show in the royal suite in just a few minutes. After floating ten bucks to the dish monkey in the kitchen, the kid had agreed to send the food up to the lobby for him at the appropriate time so he could then deliver it to the suite.

Slipping on his loafers, Vincent took a quick gulp of the remaining cold coffee in his thermos-top cup and shuddered. He began to stand, then sat back down again. The room felt a little bit rubbery, and he decided to wait for it to settle down a moment before attempting his journey to the lobby.

Maybe he shouldn't have put so much Ballentine's in his 'deluxe' coffee this year. Well, hopefully, Schreck wouldn't notice.

DaCosta took a deep breath, then stood and aimed himself through the office archway and moved toward the imposing front desk. Feeling wobbly again, he leaned heavily on the thick oak when he arrived. Across the way, Tommy Dorfman was locking the double entry doors to the Snowdrop Lounge. Though he was supposed to close at midnight, it seemed he was pulling up stakes a little early tonight. Vincent still had six hours to go on the other hand. With a sigh, he nodded across the lobby toward the bartender.

Unfortunately for Vincent, the front desk staff, which usually worked eight-hour shifts, switched over to twelve-hour shifts for the Christmas season. This allowed an extra person to take some time off over the holidays, something especially important for staff with families. The resort was relatively quiet at this time of year, except for the upcoming party on New Year's Eve in the grand ballroom. With no skiing or other winter activities apart from snowshoeing in the nearby forest, it was mostly indoor activities only at this mountaintop retreat in the wintertime — and a snoozefest, just like tonight.

Pocketing his keyring after locking the doors, Dorfman nodded back, saying, "Not much of a night, eh, Vinnie?"

The wind rattled the office windows at his back as if in agreement with Dorfman. DaCosta shook his head slightly, not about the night, but about the name the barman had used. He hated it when the bartender called him that. His full name was more formal and apropos of his job as front desk night manager, much more so than Vinnie. The name Vinnie evoked images of an underworld gangster. However, as Vincent, he shared the same first name with one of his favourite horror actors, the inimitable Vincent Price. If only he got the same respect as that master thespian did, he reflected sadly. He shook his head at Dorfman, saying, "It's as boring as hell, just like last year." With growing concern, he noted how difficult it had been to say the words 'just' and 'like' without slurring his speech — not a good thing when he still had six hours left on his shift.

Dorfman responded, "I can't believe the drink order that these guys put in. I told you how they sat in the lounge all afternoon and evening drinking vodka straight up, right?"

"Yeah, you said they drink like Frank and his pack when they visit."

"Yeah, well, unlike Peter, Sammy, and Dean, none of Schreck's pack ever seemed to get drunk. And they never ate any of the bowls of chips or peanuts from the bar, nothing at all. I know they didn't smuggle any food inside, and the kitchen never sent any orders up for them. When they all followed your buddy in the bowler hat like good little dogs over to the elevator, did they seem drunk from what you saw?"

"Nope. Not at all. Just weird and creepy."

"I know, go figure. And guess what? They ordered some more booze for midnight as well. I'm just going to run it up to them before heading out!"

"Really? How much?"

Tommy stepped over to a potted pine bedecked with twinkling Christmas lights. He wheeled out an ornate bar cart from behind it. "Here you go, look for yourself." He pushed the cart toward Vincent, and it shot smoothly across the lobby on well-oiled casters, the bottles inside jingling musically. DaCosta intercepted the cart before it could go rolling its merry way down the staircase to the kitchen. He opened the door to the wheeled cabinet. Inside, almost every imaginable brand of vodka or grain alcohol that the hotel carried was on display. Curiously, there was no rum, rye, or gin, just dozens of vodka bottles along with several bottles of Everclear thrown in for good measure. "What in God's name are they going to do, preserve scientific specimens?" Vincent asked, slurring the last couple of words.

Dorfman added helpfully, "Or scrubbing down the suite for an operation? I don't know, but I wondered about that too. I mean, how much booze can seven guys drink in the course of one night? There are three dozen bottles inside that cart. The buggers cleaned out my whole stock. That's over five bottles of booze per guy, and some of these are forty pounders! I don't know how they're going to function in their 'business meeting' if they drink all this. And speaking of which, how are you functioning at the moment, Vinnie? You don't look so hot." He crossed the lobby toward Vincent.

Having closed the liquor cabinet doors, DaCosta stood, leaning on the wheeled cart for support. The lobby had just started getting rubbery again. "Just tired," he lied.

"Yeah, I can see that." Dorfman said, grabbing the cart's handle and removing Vincent's crutch, forcing him to stand unsteadily upright. Sniffing the air, the barkeep added, "And I can smell that, too." He reached into his pants pocket and pulled out a small white canister the size of a roll of nickels and tossed it to DaCosta. Vincent caught it after a couple of bouncing tries and peered at the label as Tommy said, "Better have a blast of Binaca, buddy."

Dorfman wheeled the cart across the lobby to the elevator, pressing the call button when he arrived. The elevator pinged almost immediately, its elaborate iron gate rattling aside as the inner doors opened. He pushed the cart into the cramped elevator and turned, pulling a hundred-dollar bill from his pocket. Holding it up between his index fingers, he gave the bill a quick snap, saying "They're creepy, but they tip well!" He pressed a button on a panel inside, and the doors slid shut on Tommy's grinning face.

"That they do," DaCosta said to the empty lobby. He looked at his watch. It was now ten minutes before midnight. He retreated to the office and began spritzing his mouth with the bottle of minty-smelling Binaca from Dorfman. The alcohol base in the breath freshener caused him to look longingly at his thermos for a moment, but he knew it was empty. Despite his previous reservations regarding his drinking, he wished he were going to deliver the drink cart rather than the food cart — he sure could use another drink before seeing Schreck in the royal suite.

Vincent charted an unsteady course across the lobby to the elevator. Halfway across, a ping rang out. The lift had arrived right on time. Its doors opened, revealing a serving cart piled high with food and nobody in attendance to keep an eye on it. It looked like the kid he'd paid had taken him at his word and just rolled the car into the elevator, pressed 'L' and sent it up. Vincent had expected the boy to at least accompany it up to the lobby. He shook his head, kids these days.

The ride up to the third floor seemed to take longer than usual. With a smirk, DaCosta thought that perhaps it was because he was drunker than usual tonight. Vincent hadn't bothered looking at the menu that Schreck had passed to him and had simply handed it off to the kitchen staff. He figured now would be a great time to peek under some of the chromed serving domes and see what Schreck and his band of merry men were having for a midnight snack. He lifted the first lid, thinking it would probably be either cheese, crackers, fruit, or luncheon meat — the usual stuff.

What was revealed to his disbelieving eyes was entirely different than his expectations. Each new thing was more disgusting than the last. Raw salmon with the head still attached, bloody roasts of meat, uncooked sausage, bowls of fish roe, and glasses filled with dozens of egg yolks hid beneath the gleaming domes. He knew that there were cultures that ate a lot of protein, like the people of Northern Canada, the Inuit. But, from what he knew of his cousins to the north, Schreck and Boys definitely didn't look Inuit. He doubted if any of them could make an igloo if their life depended on it, but then again, neither could he. And although he knew that the Inuit ate raw whale blubber, this took things to a whole new level of disgusting. His feelings of queasiness and unease returned now, or maybe they'd just never left in the first place. He checked his watch. It was 11:57 P.M.

The elevator arrived on the third floor with a ding, and the doors whisked open.

Vincent looked up from his watch and flinched backward in surprise.

Standing immediately next to the elevator door was Tommy Dorfman, with one hand grasping the ornate brass railing next to it, as if for support. He said nothing and merely stared at DaCosta, a blank expression on his face — or blanker than usual, at least.

"Sweet Jesus! You scared the crap out of me, Dorfman!" His heart was hammering in his chest. With a wheeze, he added, "You can't do that stuff to me, I have a weak heart, you know!" What was this idiot up to now? He shook his head in disgust. The bartender was always going for a laugh no matter what the cost to anybody around him. Playing along, Vincent said, "Okay, what's the gag this time? Are you in some sort of holiday trance now after too many shots of eggnog from Schreck?"

Dorfman didn't respond, remaining mute and expressionless. Vincent shook his head and wheeled the cart off the elevator. He half-expected the barman to try and scare him as he passed, but Tommy continued to stand next to the railing, unmoving and only watched him as he passed, saying nothing.

Vincent kept pushing the cart, choosing now to ignore the ignoramus instead. He heard the elevator door close at his back and begin to descend and hoped it was also taking the bartender and his stupidity to where it belonged, the ground floor. He sighed and continued to push the cart down the hall, saying quietly, "Have a Merry Ho-Ho, Tommy, and a Feliz Navidad, too."

The wheels of the cart squeaked slightly as DaCosta moved down the corridor. Apparently, they weren't as well-oiled as the bar cart that Dorfman had brought up. In fact, now that Vincent looked more closely at what he was pushing, the cart didn't look like any he'd seen anyone using in room service at any time in recent memory. The kitschy design of the cart screamed of Art Deco's last gasp from the early 1940's. Vincent had been at the hotel for longer than he'd cared to remember, and nothing like this had been used to transport food since he'd been here.

It was drafty in the hallway, and he shivered. Perhaps a guest on this floor had left a window open in one of the suites he had passed. But who would do that tonight? It was definitely not the kind of night to sleep with one's windows open for fresh air, not with the current sub-zero temperatures outside and all. Vincent had almost convinced himself that that was the case and began mentally reminding himself to check for drafts at the suite's doors on his way back. And then he suddenly recalled no other guests were booked here on the third floor tonight. Schreck and his gang of sombre suits were the only residents in this part of the hotel.

The corridor seemed so much longer than he remembered. He'd finally made it to the halfway point, but it was taking forever to get there. He figured maybe that was the booze screwing with his perception — it had happened before. A small table with a pair of matching chairs was located halfway along the corridor, for those guests unable to travel its long distances all at once, he supposed. He was almost tempted to use it himself, but because of the two-hundred-dollar tip that Schreck had paid him, he wasn't about to sit down on the job.

DaCosta looked over his shoulder, checking to see the hallway wasn't stretching away for miles into the distance at his back like he felt it was. And then he did a double take.

At the opposite end of the corridor, Tommy Dorfman continued to stare back at him like an idiot. His fingers were no longer clasping the railing but now intertwined in the elaborate leaf motif metalwork that made up the outer cage of the open-air, wrought-iron elevator. DaCosta pushed forward past the chair and table, shaking his head in wonder. The barman was one of those people who loved to beat a dead horse and run a gag on far too long.

The cart continued to squeal and squawk as Vincent moved, sounding for all the world like a murder of crows circling high above his head, harbingers portending his forthcoming doom, now and forevermore. He shuddered at the thought, realising he had to stop watching so many Corman-Price flicks at the drive-in movie theatre in Entwistle — his mind was getting carried away with itself.

Vincent pressed his ear to the closed door of the royal suite and listened for a moment. He'd expected to hear a party going on inside the suite after the big boozy delivery Dorfman had just made. But there was no sound at all for some reason. He knocked loudly and called out, "Room service!" After not being bid entry right away, DaCosta turned to look over his shoulder while he waited.

In seconds that seemed to last minutes, he watched Tommy Dorfman turn around and proceed to climb onto the edge of the railing. He stood there, facing Vincent, his back to the three-story drop. What in God's name was this idiot doing, Vincent wondered. Had he gone insane or just been imbibing in too much of the stuff he pushed in the lounge? He'd never thought Dorfman was an alcoholic. Himself, maybe, but not family man Tommy Dorfman. Perhaps he was strung out on drugs and smoking some of that Mary Jane he'd heard the younger kids on the staff talking about the other day.

Sounding a million miles away, the grandfather clock in the lobby started its twelve o'clock dirge, signalling the beginning of Christmas Day. At his back, the door to the suite whisked open. Vincent snapped his head around to see Max Schreck towering behind him. His bowler hat was still perched at a jaunty angle on his head, but his face contained something else entirely new. A wickedly cruel smile curled his lips, almost spiralling inward at the corners it was so extreme — he was the Grinch made real. The suite behind him lay in blackness. He looked downward at DaCosta, saying, "Why, Vincent! How fabulous to see you! This is absolutely perfect timing. We have so been looking forward to having you! Thank you for being so punctual." He stepped aside as a pair of pale, bony arms reached out from the darkness behind him and pulled the cart into the darkened room at his back. Schreck ignored this, his undivided attention now on DaCosta.

Vincent smiled weakly and said, distractedly, "You're welcome, sir." After a slight pause, he added, "Say, Mr. Schreck, was the man that delivered the alcohol to you just a few minutes ago acting strange in any way?"

"What man?" Schreck questioned. He looked over Vincent's head down the corridor. "Oh, you mean that man? Don't you worry about him." Schreck waggled his long fingers dismissively down the hall as if he were waving bye-bye to a small child.

Vincent looked back over his shoulder. He blinked in disbelief. Dorfman was still doing his high-wire act and standing on the railing, but now he was leaning backward out over the lobby's cavernous space. Tommy's right hand was white-knuckled from grasping the cage's ornamental metalwork so tightly. The sharp-cornered leaves in its design cut into his palm and blood flowed freely down his arm. His left hand formed an imaginary gun, and his arm moved slowly and jerkily toward his temple, as if it were insanely heavy, or moving against his will. With a final terrified and imploring look, Tommy Dorfman pulled his hand-gun's invisible trigger and released his grasp from the wire cage, dropping down out of sight. Moments later, the sickening sound of soft flesh and hard bone meeting cold, Italian marble echoed up from the lobby floor far below.

"Oh my God!" DaCosta said, turning to move back down the lobby to see if he could somehow assist the bartender.

Schreck's voice rasped behind him, "Oh, I'm so sorry, my boy. God can't help him now, or you either, for that matter." Iron hands clamped down onto Vincent's thin shoulders. He was yanked backward into the darkened room, the door pounding shut in its frame behind him.

A single, brown penny loafer lay on its side outside in the hall next to a small white cannister of Binaca spray. After a moment, the heavy door opened a crack. A pallid, emaciated arm crept out and grabbed the loafer and spray. At the same time, another thin arm reached out and placed a 'Do Not Disturb' sign on the knob. The door closed once again, this time silently, in keeping with the night.

CHAPTER NINETEEN

December 24th, 2021 0905 hours

The stairs definitely appeared cleaner on Lively's second trip to the basement. As Minerva had observed, whatever was going on in this building was working its way up from the basement and accelerating. At the water halfway down, he paused. Something was wrong — at least, more so than usual around here, he mentally corrected himself.

Part of his job with CSIS had consisted of finding out where people hid things. It wasn't that he was psychic per se — usually, he just got a feeling about things being off sometimes, no doubt thanks to his hidden talents bubbling through to the surface on occasion. And right now, was one of those occasions.

In several buildings over the years, Lively had discovered hidden passages leading to secret rooms where the miscreants often hid the evidence of their surreptitious wrongdoings. But there was something new going on here, and he needed to make sure first. He climbed back up to the top, saying, "Let's see how you stack up." Moving slowly back down to the small landing, he counted each stair riser as he went. At the dogleg, he turned the corner and counted the rest of the way down to the basement.

Standing at the bottom of the stairwell, Lively loaded up the calculator app on his cell phone and proceeded to do some math. He shook his head and climbed back up to the small landing, looking at the wall opposite. "It just don't add up," he mused aloud, then said to the blank wall, "You have a little secret you want to share with me, don't you?"

Factoring in the stair riser height and presuming the standard building code of about fourteen feet per story, he realised the number of stairs between the main floor and the basement added up to many more than were needed. While he realised wiring, plumbing and conduits could take a bit of room between floors, it wouldn't usually take up almost an extra eight feet of floor space. And besides, he had factored that into his calculations already. He was pretty sure this gap between the floors, wasn't for anything to do with regular building maintenance since most hotels didn't usually hide entire rooms from view unless there was a reason they didn't want them found.

The wall appeared normal enough, not looking in any way different from most of the other walls in this hotel. But he knew looks could most definitely be deceiving around here. He pressed along the edge of the wall in various spots, trying to find a pressure point to release a latch somewhere, but had little success.

"Hmm, if someone's arms were full and they wanted to pop into a secret door, maybe a little game of footsie would be in order then?" Lively started tapping the toe of his sneaker along the baseboard where the landing met the wall. With a 'click', a small gap appeared in the corner. He pressed on the wall just above the opening and the opposite side revolved outward. "Now that is a nice touch." Lively pushed forward into the hidden space. At his back, the door completed its revolution and closed, leaving him in blackness.

Without any airflow for such a long period, it smelled stale and heavy with age inside here. In a brilliant flash of light, Lively switched on his mini-LED. A concrete corridor was revealed, which he followed to a particularly strange looking door. At first, he thought it was made of silver, but he could see it was actually brushed aluminum as he got closer. Pulling a small, black, puck-sized case from his bag, he popped it open. The arrow on the compass inside was pointing due north. Considering the length of the corridor at his back, this doorway would have to be just about directly underneath the main doors to the grand ballroom upstairs. He tried the handle, and it opened easily.

Probing the room with his light, Lively said, "Well, this is unexpected but very interesting." This was so much more than just a hidden maintenance room. It appeared as if an entirely separate level existed between the main floor and the basement. In his experience, most hotels didn't hide something like this, unless they didn't want it to be found.

It was as large, if not larger, than the grand ballroom above, but with a much lower ceiling. Everywhere he looked, thick sheets of gleaming aluminum lined the walls and floor, but not in the centre of the room, nor the ceiling above. This room had to have been built when the hotel was constructed, but to what end? Why hide an extra floor like this? He shone the light around and saw several electrical switches to one side of the door, and he flipped them upward. One after the other, bank after bank of overhead lights came on, revealing a vast, windowless room.

In the middle, a depression in the floor revealed what looked to be a satellite receiver dish from back in the eighties, but that was where the similarities ended. This dish was much larger than the ten to sixteen-foot models of that era and had to be at least forty feet across. It sloped downward into the floor about a dozen feet into what could only be described as a collector array of sorts. If someone were to fall into there, they wouldn't be climbing back out anytime soon, since the sides of the dish looked far too slick to gain any purchase.

The area overtop the dish had a large and ungainly electrical apparatus attached to the ceiling: wires, tubes and relays stuck out this way and that. It looked for all the world like a Universal Pictures set decorator from the 1930s had gone insane while designing it, sticking every imaginable doohickey and gewgaw they could imagine onto the monstrosity. But that wasn't the most remarkable thing in the room — that would have to be the ceiling. While the ballroom above had a layer of hammered copper on its ceiling worth a pretty penny at current market values, the roof of this hidden room below looked to be just a little bit more valuable than that.

Lively took a penknife from his pocket, then reached up overhead and scraped at the metal in the ceiling for a moment. It was very easy to scratch and gouge. He gave out a low whistle, then said, "Well, well. I think I know what Sinclair did with some of the fortune he pulled out of the Kootenays". From corner to corner, the ceiling gleamed brilliantly above his head, covered in pure, one hundred percent gold.

In light of this turn of events, he wouldn't be surprised to find out that the holding company was far more concerned with the whereabouts of this gold rather than the people who had disappeared inside the ballroom. "If they know this gold may be hidden up here, no wonder they're suddenly anxious to know what happened so they can 'reopen' things."

However, this brought him back to the question of why Sinclair installed all of this gold in a hidden floor inside his hotel in the first place? From everything Lively had seen so far, it was not purely for investment reasons; it looked far too utilitarian for that. There was obviously much, much more to this room than met the eye, especially if one of its more minor features was a billion dollars-worth of gold bullion stuck to its ceiling.

What was this equipment doing down here? Collecting satellite transmissions from outer space? Commercial satellites didn't even exist when this hotel was constructed in 1946, not coming into existence until the mid-sixties, so he knew that couldn't be it.

Aluminum was an excellent insulator from electricity. And that seemed to be the idea behind it lining the walls and floor in this room. But the metal inside this dish was different. It looked to be silver, which, quite interestingly, was one of nature's best conducting metals. He scratched the back of his neck, lost in thought. For some reason, this all reminded him of something from high school science class, and he couldn't quite put his finger on it.

On the far side of the shining room lay another door, this one also aluminum, and it was unlocked. Massive bundles of cables exited in a conduit over its top. "Well, this looks promising, at least." A bare, concrete hall lay beyond. Sloping slightly downward, it eventually reached a switchback. Rounding this turn revealed yet another long corridor. "Man, I should have brought my pedometer with me so I could claim mileage."

Lively paused at the bottom, trying to get his bearings. He figured he must be near the kitchen by now, or perhaps even below it. Despite having eaten only an hour before, his stomach growled mightily at the thought of food, and he flirted with scoring another peanut butter and bacon sandwich while he was in the neighbourhood. And then he sighed. The only problem was, the kitchen was obviously not directly accessible from here, so he'd have to put his rumbling stomach on the back burner for the moment.

The overhead cables passed through an opening in the wall next to another door, thankfully not aluminium this time, but rather stainless steel. It squealed slightly as he opened it and shone his light inside.

"Oh, my Lord." He had found the control room.

Banks of dials and gauges filled the wall closest to him. In the centre of the room hulked an archaic mainframe computer sporting a decidedly dated reel to reel magnetic tape storage system. Directly ahead, in a low console along the other side of the room, a row of antiquated CRT computer monitors lay shiny and dark. This place had been sealed tightly for many years with no airflow, and a lack of dust was expected, but still, it was eerily clean in here.

Another room lay in darkness beyond this one, barely visible through a large observation window inset in the wall over the monitors. Lively hit a large red button labelled 'Power Main', and dim, red lights began to flicker on inside the control room, gradually coming to life after a multi-decade hibernation. At his back, the reel-to-reel magnetic storage of the mainframe computer began to spin, click, and whir. He turned on several CRT displays on the console in front of him. The monitor on the left connected to an EEG, its screen blank. Next to it, the heart rate line of an EKG display currently ran flat. "Doesn't look like the patient made it, doctor," he said, smiling at his joke. He flicked another switch, this one labelled, 'Operating Theatre'. Bright, white lights came alive in the room beyond the viewing window.

His smile was replaced by an expression of shock. As the lights powered up, a man appeared to stare back at Lively from the other side of the glass, a broad grin on his face.

Stepping back several feet, Lively's heart jumped around in his chest from the sudden jolt of adrenaline. After blinking his eyes rapidly from the brightness as well as surprise, he saw the man in the window was gone. And then it occurred to him that the man he'd seen was not a stranger, after all, but in fact, had been his own reflection once again. However, when he'd seen it this time, he'd hardly recognised it. The other Lively's expression had been even more bizarre than last night, smiling back at him like the Mad Hatter getting ready for his tea party on the other side of the looking glass.

CHAPTER TWENTY

December 24th, 2021 0926 hours

After her initial Limey in the lobby, Minerva hadn't been paying too much attention to the details around her as she'd climbed to the royal suite. But now, she stood at the base of the ornamental staircase leading to the Sinclair's upper floors and took it all in. Without Lively egging her along, she now had the luxury of some time to further study the amazing details inside this hotel.

Rich, red oak accented by brass and rosewood inlays, accented by colourful stained glass made it a sight to behold. As Lively had noted, it seemed as if the RMS Titanic had been rebuilt here in the heart of British Columbia's rugged Coastal Mountain Range, and it now floated amongst a sea of trees instead of rusting on the seafloor of the North Atlantic. Minerva could almost see the ladies in their beautiful ball gowns, holding onto the arms of sharply dressed, handsome men in their tuxedos, as they descended the Sinclair's main staircase for a lovely evening in the breathtaking grand ballroom below.

Arriving at the first-floor mezzanine, Minerva stopped and peered intently at the massive painting overlooking the lobby. A small, engraved brass plaque underneath the portrait read, 'The Sinclair Resort Hotel in Springtime'. "Well, I'd never have guessed," she said, moving closer to inspect the amazing detail that the artist had achieved.

The obscenely large painting was attached to the wall with heavy-duty steel cables to help support its enormous weight. Minerva was sure that if it ever fell off the wall, it would do more than just make a small thud, and she wouldn't want to be anywhere nearby if it did. She measured it out by pacing along the floor in front of it. At just over eighteen feet long and ten feet high, the painting was the first thing you saw when you came into the lobby of the hotel. Apparently, they wanted to remind you of where you were, just in case you'd forgotten on your short walk in from seeing the building in real life as you came through the front doors.

The artist's ability was exceptional and the level of detail phenomenal, almost like it had been photographed, instead of painted. Minerva marvelled as she looked inside the miniature hotel's windows, admiring the detail. Outside it was a beautiful landscape of lush green forest, bright blue sky and jagged, snow-capped mountains.

Lively was correct, with the dense swirl of foliage in the woods outside and the detail in the hotel's windows, this painting definitely seemed similar to one of Martin Handford's 'Where's Waldo' challenges.

Minerva looked into the painting's woods to see if the artist had painted any indigenous fauna to go with the flora, and sure enough, she saw a bear peeking out of the trees on the left side of the hotel. The beast looked very large compared to the forest around it, and it also appeared very hungry. Over on the right side of the monumental canvas was more of the beautiful woods. In the background, peering through some bushes, was a lone wolf. Its long face appeared sly with intent as it watched a small boy playing ball with an even smaller mottled grey dog next to the vibrantly coloured forest. She said to the painted boy, "You've got company, my friend. Keep an eye out, or you and your little dog could end up as somebody's snack." With a shake of her head, she added, "Maybe they should have called this painting 'The Watchers in the Woods' instead." She stepped back, admiring the painting a bit longer, and then continued her climb to the third floor and the royal suite.

Minerva gasped, startled, as she stepped to the top of the last stair riser before the second floor, thinking she'd spied someone across the spacious room staring back at her. But as she moved the rest of the way up to floor-level, she realised she'd forgotten about the mirrors scattered across the expanse of the second-floor common area. Their strategic placement made the room appear much larger than it actually was, and created numerous reflected doppelgangers, depending on where you stood.

At the top of the third-floor staircase, portraits of three very intense-looking men resided. They were definitely not as lovely as the people in the huge painting on the mezzanine that had entranced her moments before. The middle portrait depicted the hotel's namesake, Thomas Sinclair, flanked by portraits of his two sons, Edward, and Matthew. None of the men smiled in their paintings. "You would think with the money that you guys had, you'd have at least a glimmer of a smile on one of those serious-looking mugs," Minerva said. Looking at the portrait of Thomas, she added, "And where's the portrait of your wife? Very misogynistic," Minerva observed with a tsk-tsk.

Thomas Sinclair glared back at her, stern and unforgiving. His Scottish heritage showing through in his bushy red hair that seemed to float around his head like a hazy halo. However, the face behind the halo was anything but angelic. In the portrait on the left, Matthew had a little less anger in his face, but had the same, red, most likely bushy hair, though it was harder to tell as it was slicked down and parted in the centre, as was the style of the time.

Edward Sinclair was another matter altogether. "How did any of the guests ever make it past you on the way up these stairs?" Minerva asked, looking into the piercing eyes that seemed to be the predominant feature of Edward's handsome face and chiseled jawline. Wavy reddish-brown hair and a neatly trimmed moustache completed his look, making him appear remarkably similar to a famous actor of the time, Errol Flynn. "You must have been quite a hit with the ladies, I'll say that much."

She slowly moved past the portraits and watched as the portrait's eyes seemed to follow her. Thanks to her stunning appearance, Minerva was used to the gaze of men upon her. It usually didn't bother her, but the way these portraits glared at her made her uncomfortable. With a small shrug, she said, "Well, I should've figured that would've been a given in a place like this."

At the far end of the long corridor lay the door to the royal suite. Before exploring further, Minerva wanted to check out some of the information Lively had gleaned from his reports and interviews about the third floor. A nearby conversation seat covered in rich, embroidered red silk looked like a comfortable spot to read. Taking a handkerchief from her backpack, she placed it on the dusty seat, then sat down and cracked open her copy of the Big Book of Ballroom Busting. It was time to check into the royal suite.

***

Throughout the 1950s and 1960s, the Sinclair's royal suite had been host to dozens of high-level politicians, royalty and celebrities. Rob Ruby was one such celebrity, a well-known host of a popular game show taped in Vancouver called, 'You Bet Your What?'

Rob Ruby also had a penchant for younger women and was a notorious womaniser, dating starlet after starlet, some already married and some not, it didn't matter to him. This particularly beautiful fall afternoon in October 1965, Ruby was hosting a little get together of his own with the very married wife of his executive producer, Sonny Wright.

Isabelle Wright had been in the middle of a passionate afternoon delight with Rob when her husband, Sonny had come knocking with both fists on the royal suite's front door. When Sonny Wright finally came through that door, he did not turn the handle. In fact, he quite literally came through the door, bringing most of the surrounding frame with him in the process.

Sonny Wright was Rob Ruby's producer on 'You Bet Your What?' But many years before that, Sonny had also been a professional wrestler and bodybuilder. Standing six-feet-seven inches tall and sporting three-hundred and twenty-five pounds of solid muscle, Sonny was a moving slab of a man. Like a side of lean beef with legs, not an ounce of his frame was allocated to fat. He was the kind of man whose muscles seemed to have their own muscles when he clenched his fists.

The front desk manager had reported that Wright had been in such a hurry when he stormed through the main doors, that he had almost flown across the lobby. And then he'd purportedly mounted the grand staircase taking a nearly impossible three steps at a time with each stride of his long, muscular legs.

The only reason that Wright still had anything to do with Ruby at this point in his career was because of the money involved. Between the two of them, they'd made a lot of it. Starting out as friends many years before, Sonny produced for Rob on a couple of shows back in the late 1950s with moderate success. When 'You Bet Your What?' premiered in early 1961, the show had taken off. Now, the simple fact of the matter was that Sonny simply made too much money producing Ruby's show to even consider giving up the partnership.

Working with Ruby, Sonny Wright had made the kind of money to which neither he, nor Isabelle could say no, especially since they needed it so badly. Isabelle's exorbitant spending habits and Sonny's own experimental foray into steroidal drug use had added to their cash flow woes. But it turned out there was an additional thing that Isabelle couldn't say no to, and that was Rob Ruby's sexual advances.

But something big had come along that had changed things for everyone — life-changing for some, and life-ending for others. When Sonny learned of Isabelle's infidelity, his anger had been huge, but when he discovered who she'd been cheating on him with, it had gone supernova.

Rob Ruby had been insanely popular for many years and had what seemed a cult-like following all his very own. He could have had any woman he'd ever wanted, but he, or perhaps the little thinker between his legs, had decided it was a good idea to seduce Sonny Wright's gorgeous wife instead.

Isabelle was as beautiful as she was untouchable. Any man who had ever flirted with her had been in a very sorry state the next day, collecting either a black eye, a broken arm, or both for their interest. Another thing that added to Sonny's expenses were the constant lawsuits caused by his incessant jealousy.

Almost everyone knew you'd be signing your own death warrant if you tried to get it on with Isabelle Wright. Sonny had even reportedly said to Rob at one time, if he ever found out about any guy screwing his wife, well, that guy wouldn't need to worry about living for very much longer.

For whatever reason, Ruby decided not to heed those words of warning. Much like a predator that is so focused on its prey that it sometimes fails to see other potential predators or hazards nearby, so it was with Rob Ruby and his advances on Isabelle Wright. When Rob had laid his predatory eyes on Isabelle, he'd seemingly forgotten that he was toying with the wife of a man so large his muscles required an extra seat on the airplane whenever he travelled.

This mass of muscles now plowed through the royal suite's locked bedroom door, leaving nothing but wooden fragments in its wake.

It seemed Sonny was in a hurry to redecorate the royal suite with some lovely new fall colours that he was just itching to try out — colours that featured bright splashes of crimson and a heavy emphasis on black and blue.

Outside the hotel, on that beautiful fall afternoon in October 1965, the sun was shining, and what few leaves remained on the trees, fluttered to the ground in the light, crisp breeze. Overhead, a V of Canada geese flew south for the winter, their plaintive cries mingling with the blood-curdling screams that rang out from the top floor of the Sinclair Resort Hotel.

CHAPTER TWENTY-ONE

December 24th, 2021 1011 hours

Lively's breathing seemed louder inside his head than usual. But this seemed to go hand in hand with his accelerated heart rate, which wasn't unexpected. The door leading into the operating theatre lay just up ahead, and he moved slowly toward it.

He was fairly certain his eyes hadn't been playing tricks. But he decided not to take any chances and moved cautiously nonetheless, in case there actually was a person lying in wait, just out of sight beneath the viewing window — someone who looked an awful lot like him. With a slow turn of the knob, he clicked the door open and peered into the room.

"Anybody home?"

The theatre room remained mute to his inquiry, unable to verify its current occupancy, but it looked to be empty. An operating table lay in its centre, but there was something 'off' about it. It was coated in white porcelain like a bathtub. A large drain was located at one end, and a shallow gutter ran around the circumference of the table's raised edges. And then it dawned on him; this wasn't an operating table; this was an embalming table.

"What? Why on earth would they need an embalming table in a hotel?" Off to one side of the table sat a rack containing a series of bizarre devices, not dissimilar to the crazy looking apparatus overtop of the dish in the golden room. "What were you guys doing in here? Trying to make like Jeffery Combs and reanimate the dead?"

There was a tall, white medicine cabinet in the far corner of the room. Thanks to the large pane of glass that took up most of the front of the cabinet, he could see it contained a variety of drugs. "This looks well stocked for just about every emergency."

One of the many positions Lively had held through his work for CSIS was that of an interrogator. However, he abhorred using violent or cruel interrogation methods on anyone and preferred instead to question his subjects under controlled circumstances. Thanks to his natural ability to suss things out from a person, he rarely used any drugs during an interrogation. But there was the odd occasion when a suspect was less than forthcoming with their information. Then, and only then, would Lively pump them full of powerful, mind-altering drugs.

He opened the cabinet, feeling like a kid in a candy store. The top shelf contained vials of morphine, oxycodone, fentanyl, and other potent pain medications. On the next shelf down, bottles labelled lysergic acid diethylamide sat next to tinctures of THC, which were just across from several large bottles of ether. Psilocybin extract from magic mushrooms sprouted on the shelf below and in one corner he discovered several glass vials of sodium thiopental and ketamine. Nodding in satisfaction, Lively smiled as he picked up a vial of thiopental, saying, "Looks like the truth has been inside this cabinet all along! I'll have to let David Duchovny know once we get things resolved around here." He placed the vial in his jacket pocket, then scooped several more vials of each drug into his hands and placed them into a large side pocket in his messenger bag. "Because you just never know." He closed the cabinet door and patted the cabinet's side as he moved away toward the far corner of the room, saying, "Keep those diamonds up in the sky for Lucy, my friend."

A door in the corner exited the room, and he decided to carry on through to wherever this maze of hidden corridors came out. Another long hallway lay before him, this one was quite dim. A musty scent filled his nostrils, and Lively felt like he was going to sneeze again.

More cables and piping ran along the ceiling, exiting through various shafts into other parts of the hotel. Where did those go, he wondered. Were there other areas around this hotel that were somehow connected to whatever had been in the gold room?

A sudden noise caused him to turn in surprise. He shone his light down the dim hall at his back and saw nothing. "Must be getting a little jumpy here." He continued forward, and within a few seconds, the noise came to him again. It was a skittering noise, like something small and light moving quickly and surreptitiously in the dark, shadowing his movements. He paused once more and listened intently.

Nothing. No sound.

After a couple more hesitant steps forward, he heard the noise again. This time he was able to detect the direction from which it came and aimed his light up into the piping and conduits overhead.

"Gah!" Lively pulled back against the wall of the corridor with an adrenalised jolt. He moved sideways a few feet, never taking his light off of what had been perched above his head.

Eight dark eyes regarded him from atop a sizeable conduit near the ceiling of the tunnel. Attached to those dark, shiny eyes were eight, long, hairy legs belonging to one of the most massive wolf spiders he had ever seen. There weren't many things in this world of which a man the size of Lively was afraid. But spiders just happened to be one of those things that freaked him out to no end. And ones that had bodies the size of dinner plates like the one perched on the pipe made him feel even more panicked.

He couldn't imagine how he would have reacted if the creature had dropped down onto him from overhead without warning as it stalked him. He shivered as he thought of the spiky little leg hairs that covered the creature's long, spindly legs wrapping around his neck or his head. "Man, you are one homely not-so-little dude," he said to the spider, as he sidled another foot or two along the wall in the opposite direction from it, just in case.

The large arachnid regarded him without moving, the flashlight's beam reflecting off its multiple sets of eyes. After what seemed like a very long time, the creature began to move along the pipes once more toward the corridor's end. Lively had a choice to make since the hallway branched into a 'T' intersection here. "Okay, which way now?" he asked the arachnid. It scuttled down the branch to the left, and Lively followed it at a safe distance. Another closed door stood at the end of this short hallway. Near the door, he glimpsed the spider scuttling up into a gap in the ceiling cut for an electrical conduit.

Lively edged toward the doorway, shining his light up into the space where the spider had moved, but there was no further sign of the creature. He was still on edge, ready for the beast to pounce on him as if he were some unsuspecting prey destined for one of its silken cocoons.

The door had no doorknob, but rather a handle meant for sliding it sideways to open. Giving the handle a good hard pull to the side, Lively paused. He blinked several times rapidly in the bright light that flooded from the open doorway. Stepping through the opening, Lively turned around and saw that the other side of the door was a shelf lined with boxes. He slid the door closed and smiled. It once more looked like heavily laden shelving resting against the concrete wall behind it. To the rack, he said, "I wonder what other little secrets are scattered around this hotel behind innocent-looking shelves like you?"

Turning slowly around, Lively swept the space with his questing flashlight revealing a large storage room. Tall metal shelves lined both sides of the elongated space. Despite being only fifteen feet wide or so, it ran about sixty feet long in the other direction. Another row of shelves ran down the middle, separating the room into two halves. The shelves were stacked floor to ceiling with boxes of all shapes and sizes, all labelled by someone's tidy hand in black grease pencil.

To his right were located several boxes with 'Lost & Found' on them. Lifting the lid on the first box, Lively peered inside. Apart from some eyeglasses, a pair of dentures and a few books, there didn't seem to be anything of much interest. He decided to take a quick browse through a few more of these boxes just to see what there was to see.

Things were segregated into sections like he was in someone's basement looking through their decades of stored bric-a-brac. One section almost a dozen feet long was labelled Christmas Decorations, followed by shorter areas marked Halloween, Thanksgiving, Easter and more. These shelves seemed to contain boxes dedicated to every holiday decoration scheme, almost. "What? No Hanukkah, Ramadan, or Kwanzaa? How typically North American." He shook his head sadly.

After the holidays, the seasons of the year came next. He now stood at the far end of the room browsing inside a box labelled 'Spring' when he heard a noise; a scraping sound of something rubbing slowly over something else. Suddenly, on the other side of the divided room, a box fell off the shelf, spilling its contents onto the floor.

"Hello?" Lively said. He was standing at the end of the aisle and was able to take two quick steps to his right to look toward the entry door. There was no one in sight, only a cardboard carton laying on the floor halfway up the aisle. Thoughts of the spider flitted through his mind for a moment as he approached the box. He warily scanned the shelves nearby, keeping an eye out for a possible ambush by his eight-legged friend.

"Okay, so you want me to look at something, do you?" Lively asked the room as he poked the fallen carton with his toe. Nothing hairy, creepy, or crawly came out of the box, and he knelt to examine it. A Ouija board had spilled out, along with its wooden planchette and battered cardboard box, both looking to be many decades old. The wooden board had letters of the alphabet arcing in two rows across the top, with numbers in a straight row beneath. The word "Yes" was engraved in the upper left-hand corner of the board with 'No' sitting in opposition.

"This is a collector's item." He turned it over to see the back. "Whoa. Even better, it's the Canadian Copp Clark William Fuld edition!" This board was quite rare, not because of its design, but rather the story behind it. He began to put the mess on the floor back into the carton and discovered something even more interesting than the Ouija board.

Several decks of worn playing cards lay next to a snakes and ladders board game, which partially covered an old Monopoly set. Underneath all of that gaming goodness, he found a small glass orb, wrapped in an old, checkered cloth. It almost looked like a crystal ball that a medium would use, but slightly smaller, around the size of a baseball. The globe was cloudy in the centre. Lively held it up to the overhead light and peered into it. He wasn't sure, but the cloudiness at the centre of the glass seemed to be moving, ever so gradually, almost like real clouds do when you stare up at them sometimes. You know they're moving, but just going slowly enough to not be readily apparent. He wrapped it back up and put the orb inside his courier bag, along with the planchet and the Ouija board for good measure, the latter sticking out of the top of the bag. He would have Minerva look at them a little bit later and perhaps they would try them out to see if anything happened.

As he approached the entry door, he glanced at the remaining cartons' labels along the way. There were parts for the irrigation system, extra dinnerware and cutlery, pillows, blankets, and pretty much any item you'd need to restock or replace in a hotel seemed to be inside this room. Lively wrote a few notes in his notebook, then paused as a thought struck him.

He suddenly reversed his decision and his direction, thinking instead that he should see exactly where the other corridor went back there at the hidden 'T' intersection. He returned to the heavily laden shelf in front of the secret corridor and rolled it aside, saying, "Once more into the breach." Clicking on his flashlight, Lively stepped through the hidden doorway. He turned and slid the door shut, venturing once more into the hotel's underworld, its darkness consuming him completely.

CHAPTER TWENTY-TWO

December 24th, 2021 1115 hours

The door to the royal suite was currently closed, but Minerva was sure they had left it open when they'd gone for breakfast. It was a minor thing, but just another example of the little details around the hotel to which a person needed to pay attention.

Tentatively tracing her fingers along the suite's door handle, she half-expected to feel a jolt of electricity or freezing cold, but there was nothing. She let out a small breath of anticipation she'd been holding, then fully grasped the doorknob and turned it, pushing the door open once again.

Sunlight streamed through the open drapes, bathing the room in stark white light, showcasing its dated opulence. Antiques were on display everywhere. In front of her sat a pair of Louis XIV armchairs that were surely worth a small fortune just on their own. In between them, in a mishmash of centuries, sat a French Empire Gueridon table with what looked like a Ming Vase in its centre. Just another example of the money that was invested in this hotel. She could definitely see why the holding company was so interested in getting the place up and running again, instead of leaving everything gathering dust here in the mountains of BC. Minerva gave a small shake of her head — if only they hadn't ruined the look of the room with the thick, white, shag carpet that covered every square inch of the floors in the suite. She imagined that gruesome addition had come sometime in the late 1960s during a renovation refresh most likely.

Looking more closely at the furniture, Minerva could have sworn it was a lot dustier in here when she'd arrived earlier this morning. But now, it looked as if it had been covered with a cloth all these years, one that had only recently been removed. But if that were the case, she thought, there would be evidence of other spots still covered with dust, such as the white carpet, but the room seemed immaculate, almost as if the maid had wandered by a few minutes ago.

"You really are waking up, aren't you?" she asked the room nodding her head slightly. Minerva gazed into a large, framed mirror that occupied a section of the far wall. Her likeness nodded back in agreement with her observation. She stopped nodding and stared at her reflection, lost in thought. What echoes of lives lived had this glass seen over the decades?

An overwhelming urge to touch the mirror came upon her. She moved slowly toward the oversized looking glass, wondering, if she made contact with it, would she be able to step through like Alice?

The reality of her flight of fancy, she discovered, was icy cold glass, like a jar from just out of the freezer. With a short intake of breath, she pulled away for a moment, rubbing her fingertips together, feeling the flesh chilled to the bone. The glass was almost painful to touch, but she didn't want to put on any gloves and lessen the contact with its surface. The brief moment she'd just experienced had been more than enough to tell her there was much more to this mirror than met the eye. She closed her eyes and cleared her thoughts. After a moment, she touched the mirror again.

Echoes of life resonated through her fingertips, flooding up her arm and into her mind with a kaleidoscope of images and sensations. Millions upon millions of 'moments' swirled through her head. Brief snippets of people and the things they had done throughout the day, and the night, while staying here in the royal suite. Echoes of love and passion, pleasure and pain, joy and heartbreak, and lust and horror. It was that last echo from the mirror that was strongest of all.

"Okay, that's enough." Minerva withdrew her hand from the mirror. She needed to know more but needed a break, saying, "Let's finish this little story first." She pulled out Lively's manuscript once more, wanting to finish the last page of the Sonny Wright saga that she still had to read. But before she did that, she wanted to move her reading into the room where the event happened, the royal suite's bedroom. From everything she'd read up until

Sonny broke into the suite, it certainly sounded like that fall day five and a half decades ago had ended in a case of domestic violence and/or homicide.

It turned out she was both correct and incorrect at the same time. There was plenty of violence, but not of the domestic kind. Isabelle Wright had been found naked in the centre of the round king-sized bed, her eyes wide and staring, unable to utter a word. The room around her had been in complete disarray as if a tropical storm had blown through in the middle of the afternoon. In a way, it had, and the storm's name had been Sonny Wright.

When hotel staff arrived soon after the fracas, no sign of Sonny or Rob had been found. Something extremely violent had occurred in the suite, of that there was no doubt, and it had left Isabelle an emotionally damaged vegetable for the rest of her life. However, no blood or bodily fluids were ever found anywhere in the room, something that surely would have been expected in a fight in which Sonny Wright had been involved.

The official RCMP report came back that there had been signs of a struggle, and that indeed, someone may have been hurt, but no one knew where either man had gone, and Isabelle Wright wasn't talking. She never said another word after that day, spending the rest of her life, semi-comatose, in a small room at Vancouver's Sunnybrae Mental Institution. They had tried drugs, shock therapy, literally anything to get her to talk about what had happened. But nothing had worked, and she remained mute until the day she died, a little over fifty years later.

Photos from inside the suite showed massive damage to the furniture, walls, and windows. It appeared that Sonny had literally cleaned the room with Rob Ruby. Indented in the plaster of one wall, the outline of a man could be clearly seen. Scattered nearby, numerous antique chairs and tables lay in pieces. Whether they were crushed from somebody being thrown onto them or by being smashed over somebody's head, no one would ever know for sure.

No staff or guests reported seeing either of the men after that afternoon altercation. And it wasn't like the pair could have just sauntered past the front desk and out the door. Rob Ruby's fame and Sonny Wright's physique were two factors that made it virtually impossible for either of them to go anywhere without being noticed. In addition, judging by the damage to the suite, just the thought of Rob Ruby walking out of the Sinclair Hotel of his own volition would have been an act of purest optimism. Neither Sonny Wright nor the object of his attention, Mr. Rob Ruby, were ever seen or heard from again.

Minerva returned to the mirror, wanting to touch its surface once more. The glass wasn't freezing cold now and..." She jerked backward in surprise several steps when the mirror began suddenly sliding aside.

The reflective glass disappeared, moving sideways into a recess on one side, leaving the intricate wooden frame still attached to the wall's exterior. Standing on the other side of the frame, posing like a full-length living portrait, was Lively.

"Hey, Sis! Welcome to Wonderland!" As he spoke, he broke his pose and poked his thumb over his shoulder toward the dim, dusty corridor at his back.

Clasping her chest slightly from surprise, Minerva said, "Lively! You scared the bejesus out of me!"

"Yeah, sorry about that. I just got here a few seconds ago when you were walking up to the mirror. Poor timing on my part I suppose," he said, smiling sheepishly, then brightened and concluded, "But you gotta check this out!" He gestured excitedly over his shoulder with his thumb once more.

"I presume you've found the March Hare or the Mad Hatter?" Minerva shook her head slightly, still feeling the adrenaline coursing through her veins.

"Well, not quite. But this is where it gets interesting, trust me!"

"It wasn't interesting already?"

"Oh yes, it certainly was. But let me just say this: you ain't seen nothin', until you've seen what lies on the other side of this looking glass, Alice. So, c'mon!" He gestured with his arm for her to follow and turned. Moving away into the dim corridor once more, he began singing the refrain from David Bowie's Golden Years as he walked.

Minerva shook her head and pulled out her flashlight. She turned it on and speared the gloom that seemed to have swallowed her brother whole, then stepped through the frame to follow his lead. Behind her, the mirror slid silently back into place, a hidden latch inside clicking closed as it did. To Minerva's jangled nerves, it sounded like a gun being cocked.

CHAPTER TWENTY-THREE

December 24th, 2021 1143 hours

Row upon row of weak incandescent lights hid behind red glass housings. "What in the world?" Minerva asked. This corridor stretched for what looked like the entire length of the hotel. There seemed to be an entire underworld behind the walls of this resort.

No longer singing David Bowie, Lively had stopped a few feet past her position in front of an unmarked door in the narrow corridor. He looked back over his shoulder, saying, "What's the matter, Sis? Not my singing, I hope?"

"Well, first of all, I don't think Michael Buble has anything to worry about. And no, it's not that, it's the lighting here. What's with the darkroom lights?"

"Isn't it something? This network of corridors runs throughout the entire hotel from what I can see, and these lights are everywhere. They're usually used in places where regular light could cause a problem, such as a dark room like you said, or perhaps in a surveillance operation."

"Surveillance operation?"

Lively pushed the door in front him open, saying, "Allow me to show you."

A large room lay beyond the unassuming door. The air had a stale smell in here like a wardrobe full of old clothes, long unopened. It was almost lounge-like, tastefully decorated with a variety of comfortable leather chairs and chaise lounges. A teakwood drink cart stood next to one wingback chair, as if ready to serve a cocktail to whoever was next waiting their turn in this hidden den of depravity, located behind this seemingly respectable hotel's walls. The chair sat facing a series of two-way mirrors.

Minerva moved toward the glass. On the other side lay the royal suite's common area, daylight streaming through its partially opened drapes.

"What is this? A lounge for peeping Toms? Or an observation room for recording and blackmailing people?"

"Oh, no, it's much more than that!" Lively led her to another door on the far side of the room and pushed it open.

"You seem to know where you're going. Is there something you're not telling me?" Minerva didn't enter the room but hung back a moment so she could ask her question, concern heavy in her voice.

"I've had a few minutes to explore since I last saw you, you know. But now that you mention it, it's strange."

"How so?"

"Well, I almost feel like I know my way around in the gloom, which is impossible since I've never been back here in my life."

"Maybe it's because you're so comfortable around surveillance situations from your time in CSIS?" Minerva suggested.

"Maybe," Lively said with a shrug. He stepped through the doorway into the new room and added, "But you've gotta check this out."

Thick soundproofing material lined the walls of this new room, giving whoever was back here the privacy they might need to fulfil some of their more secret desires, perhaps. A surgical table with straps lay in the centre of the room. "Okay, this is getting seriously creepy." She moved to the table and touched one of the straps, then yanked her hand back with an intake of breath, as if the strap were red hot. The emotions of anguish, sorrow and horror rushed through her mind, overwhelming her senses.

"What's up?" Lively turned from a cabinet he'd been inspecting, concerned.

"This table and the straps."

"I take it you sensed something?"

"Oh yeah, all sorts of different things, but none of them good." Apart from the emotions, there was something else she'd sensed, pain, overwhelming and unrelenting pain. She shuddered a little, still seeing disturbing images behind her eyes when she closed them briefly. "Remind me not to touch any more restraining straps around here, okay?" She moved away from the table and returned to the observation room with her mind awhirl.

"There's more to see, Ms. D, follow me," Lively said, moving toward the door to the corridor.

Minerva followed Lively down another long, dusty hallway working their way further into the guts of the old hotel. Her bootheels made no noise as she walked since all of the corridors were lined with thick industrial carpeting, presumably to cut down on any chance of the sound of someone walking behind the walls alerting anyone on the other side to their presence. Whoever or whatever walked behind these walls walked silently. "It certainly is well soundproofed back here," she observed.

"Yes," Lively replied, "It makes it much easier to stalk people that way."

"What a charming thought."

"I calls it as I sees it."

He led her down a wrought-iron spiral staircase to the second floor. Instead of carpeting, thick latex rubber covered these stairs to mute any sound made by the inhabitants of this netherworld as they climbed up and down. More hidden hallways branched off on both sides leading to more discreet viewing areas behind their respective two-way mirrors. While these were not as large as the 'lounge' upstairs, they all shared the same concept. Mixed in with the viewing areas dotted along the way were what she could only think of as 'emergency exits' leading into the public corridor. She tried one of them and popped her head out into the brightly lit hallway. "It looks like they could pop in and out of here whenever they wanted."

"Yup. And you know each of the mirrors you saw in those observation areas?"

"Uh-huh?"

"They all open, as well."

"Eww! So, whoever was back here could wander out in the middle of the night and watch people sleep?"

"Yes, amongst other things, I would imagine."

It seemed all aspects of the Sinclair's guest's personal lives and habits were on full display to anyone who wanted to observe them. When this hotel had been open, she wondered what went on behind the scenes here. Could the disappearance of all those people be somehow connected to these mirrors? Was everybody shuffled out of the ballroom through some secret exit down there? But that was impossible, and she knew it. No amount of hustling would have moved ninety-eight people through any doorway in fifteen seconds.

How many thousands of people had stayed here over the years unaware of this vast hidden surveillance network? It seemed that with the access that unseen people had to each of the suites in this hotel, that there was much more than met the eyes around here. What had it been used for? Blackmail, kidnappings, mysterious disappearances?

Eventually, she found herself standing at the bottom of the spiral staircase on the main floor. This corridor was quite similar to the second floor except it seemingly branched everywhere behind the walls, leading into almost every section. And there were quite a few more of the access points along these gloomy hidden halls as well. These 'emergency exits' made her uneasy. Especially now that she knew how many of them lay behind the public corridor's wall panels and mirrors. With a shiver, she supposed they made it easier for people up to various nefarious activities in the hotel to go about their business undetected. But it also made her wonder how many people just disappeared walking down the hotel corridor over the years, taken from behind, unaware of someone that had just come out of the wall at their back. Like many things around this hotel, she was coming to learn, these mirrors served a dual purpose.

"My God. Someone could move around this entire hotel without ever being seen!"

"I know! Isn't it great?" Lively seemed to be enjoying himself, at least. "But you still haven't seen the best part."

"The best part? You mean there's more?"

"But of course!" Lively led her down a short corridor, saying, "I think it was just down here."

"What's just 'down here'? A vat of hydrochloric acid, or a pit of lye?"

"No, silly rabbit, this!" He stepped aside to reveal an antiquated-looking elevator. "Step aboard!"

"What? Are you crazy? Isn't it unsafe to take an elevator around this place? You know, power outages and all?"

"I know, I thought of that, but this has an access panel on the top of the elevator car. If there's a problem, then we can just pop it open and shimmy up the cables to get out."

"Oh, is that all? Well, okay then, let's go!" Minerva said with mock enthusiasm.

"Minerva, it'll be fine," Lively counselled. "Trust me, I really don't think this hotel is out to get us."

"For the moment, at least. Besides, how do you know this elevator doesn't descend into a shaft filled with water that would drown us like rats?"

"Cause I've already taken it."

"You are crazy!"

"I only took it up from the basement to the first floor to try it out." Lively stepped into the elevator car and added, "You really need to check out the control panel in here." Seeing his sister's reluctance, he egged her on, saying, "C'mon, you know you want to."

With a sigh, Minerva stepped into the elevator. But Lively was correct, she really did want to see this control panel inside the elevator. "Huh? What are those? Where's the numbers?"

"Who needs numbers when you can use pictographs, I always say."

"You do, do you?" Minerva examined the control panel and shook her head. There were four buttons in a vertical row like usual for a three-story building with a basement. But situated in the spots that traditional numerals would have been located were what appeared to be, as Lively had observed, hieroglyphics. Sitting in the topmost position was the symbol for air. Below was what looked like fire, and the floor that they were currently on seemed to be earth. At the very bottom was a symbol of waves which she presumed to mean water. "Why wouldn't they have numbers? Were there people walking around back here that couldn't read?"

"Maybe whoever was using the elevator was unfamiliar with the Hindu-Arabic system that we use these days?"

"But it's been used in European society for about a thousand years, and for almost another millennia before that in India and the Middle East. Are you saying travellers from beyond time have been riding up and down inside this elevator?"

"I don't know what to say, except that it operates just like a regular one." With that, Lively slid the cast iron gate across the doorway. He said, "Want to have the honours?"

"I swear if this descends into water and drowns us like rats, I'll haunt you myself." Minerva pressed the button with the waves on it, and they began to descend to the basement.

The machinery that operated the elevator was very quiet. In fact, Minerva had to strain to hear it. With an almost inaudible 'clunk' they arrived in the basement.

Lively pulled the gate aside and stepped out first saying, "See? No water. No rats."

Minerva gave Lively a sisterly 'stink-eye' expression as she walked out of the elevator car. "Well, what do you know, more hidden hallways."

"But you have to see where this one goes," Lively said enigmatically and moved off down a hallway branching to the left.

Minerva followed, saying, "The water symbol was appropriate for down here. It smells so damp and musty, doesn't it?"

"Really, I hadn't noticed," Lively said with a small smile. "All right, here we are!" He opened a heavy steel door and ushered her inside. They wandered by the embalming table and drug cabinet without a second glance.

"Say, isn't that table a..."

"Yes, it is." Lively nodded.

"Gross." Minerva shivered at the thought of what may have occurred on top of the table's porcelain surface. She followed her brother into another connecting room where an old mainframe computer clicked and whirred away in its centre. Along one section of wall, dozens of dials, knobs, and gauges glowed dimly. "The power is on in here?"

"Yeah, that was me," Lively admitted. "I pushed a couple of these buttons." He pointed to several large, red power buttons running in a row. The buttons labelled 'Power Main' and 'Operating Theatre' were already activated and glowing red. Next to them, another button labelled, 'Collection Aggregator' was still dark. He added, "However, I never pressed this one. I wonder what it does?" He pressed his thumb in the centre of the button and it lit up bright red like the others, followed by what sounded like a heavy-duty relay being flipped somewhere. A visceral, low-level hum began to emanate from somewhere nearby.

"That doesn't sound too encouraging. What did you do, start the countdown for self-destruct mode?"

Lively laughed, then said, somewhat seriously, "No. I'm pretty sure we'll be okay."

"Oh, good, as long as you're pretty sure."

After a whirlwind tour of the rest of the control room, Minerva found herself in another corridor with a brightly polished aluminum door at its end. As they moved toward the door, Lively looked up, down and all around.

"What are you looking for?" Minerva asked, tilting her head slightly as she watched him.

"I made another friend the last time I was through here."

"My but you're the gregarious one! Friends everywhere, it seems!"

"Well, this little 'friend' would have had you running at ninety miles per hour in the other direction."

"What was it?"

"Ever see the movie, Arachnophobia?"

"Yes, and it creeped the hell out of me."

"Well, picture something like that, but larger."

"Okay, I don't think I need to know any more right now." Minerva said, her skin tingling with just the thought of an oversized spider sitting down beside her. She really couldn't understand how Miss Muffet could have survived on her tuffet for all those years with something like that lurking around.

"Get ready to put your shades on." Lively turned the handle and pushed the door open to show her the way.

Minerva wandered silently into the room beyond, her eyes unblinking as she took in the golden ceiling above as well as the aluminum shielding that covered everything else. The humming was louder in here and seemed to be coming from the centre of the room.

Lively steered her toward the depression where the dish was located. "It reminds me of something, how this room is designed, with these aluminum floors and that conductive gold in the ceiling."

Minerva looked up at the apparatus over the dish and said, "Where are we, exactly?"

"I was wondering if you'd ask that. We are directly beneath the grand ballroom."

Minerva stood looking at the device in the ceiling, lost in thought, then said, "That thing looks like it's straight out of Weird Science."

Lively had been staring at it silently as well, then said, "Classic movie. Good reference, Sis." After another moment, he said, "Omigod! That's it!"

"What's it?"

"I think I know what this room is," Lively said, his eyes lighting up.

"What? You've figured it out?" Minerva asked, surprised.

"Not quite, but I think thanks to you, I have a pretty good feeling about what this room is at least."

Minerva looked around once more and then back to Lively. "Well, okay, you're welcome. So, would you like to share your guess, Amazing Kreskin?"

"Well, when I first saw this thing, I thought that it reminded me of something from high school, but I couldn't quite put my finger on it." Lively walked around the collector dish while he spoke. "However, keeping in mind where we're situated, with the copper ceiling in the ballroom above and all this gold below, it's like a sandwich of super-conductivity, especially with all this aluminum shielding the room down here as well..." He trailed off, giving Minerva a chance to ponder things.

Minerva's eyes lit up as her own inner light bulb finally turned on, and she exclaimed, "This entire section of the hotel is a gigantic Faraday Cage!"

"That's a big bingo, Little Sister." Lively said, smiling and nodding, then added, "It's always nice to see you come up to speed like that."

"Hey, in my own defence, I told you I didn't have much sleep last night."

"True enough. I'll make an allowance this time." Lively grinned, then looked around the room once more. "But seriously, if this room is what we think it is, what did they use it for?" He tapped with his toe at the edge of the dish's large circumference.

Minerva was silent for a moment, then shivered slightly as a single word came to the forefront of her mind, and she said, "I think I know."

"Don't keep me in suspense, what do you think they were collecting?"

Feeling suddenly cold, Minerva clasped her arms together and shuddered this time, then said quietly, "Souls."

End of Book 1

To read ABANDONED Book 2 right now, click here:

https://amzn.to/3FdmoQL

FINAL WORDS

Thank you so much for reading ABANDONED: A Lively Deadmarsh Novel, Book 1. I hope you have enjoyed the first instalment in this brand-new series.

Please make sure to join my newsletter, The Katie Berry Books Insider, for further novel updates, free short stories, chapter previews and giveaways. To join, click here: https://katieberry.ca/become-a-katie-berry-books-insider-and-win/

Reviews are critical to a book's success. The more honest reviews a book has, the better it is for everybody, because then, we all win. You win by getting to share your enjoyment with others and introduce them to a new story, and this book series wins through gaining new readers because of the reviews from concerned and engaged people like yourself.

And so, if you would like to share your thoughts with others, please leave a review: This is a direct link to the Amazon review page for ABANDONED Book 1 so you can leave a few thoughts while everything is fresh in your memory: http://www.amazon.com/review/create-review?&asin=B08W1SN1S9

I look forward to seeing you very soon for the further adventures of Lively and Minerva in Book 2 of ABANDONED.

Good health and great reads to you all,

-Katie Berry

CURRENT AND UPCOMING RELEASES

CLAW: A Canadian Thriller (November 28th, 2019)

CLAW Emergence Novelette – Caleb Cantrill (September 13th, 2020)

CLAW Emergence Novelette – Kitty Welch - (November 26th, 2020)

CLAW Resurgence (September 30th, 2021)

CLAW Emergence Book 1 (December 24th. 2022)

CLAW Emergence Book 2 (July 1st, 2023)

CLAW Emergence Book 3 (December 24th, 2023)

CLAW Resurrection (Spring 2024)

ABANDONED: A Lively Deadmarsh Novel Book 1 (February 26th, 2021)

ABANDONED: A Lively Deadmarsh Novel Book 2 (May 31st, 2021)

ABANDONED: A Lively Deadmarsh Novel Book 3 (December 23rd, 2021)

ABANDONED: A Lively Deadmarsh Novel Book 4 (July 15th, 2022)

BESIEGED: A Lively Deadmarsh Novel (Fall 2024)

CONNECTIONS
Email: katie@katieberry.ca
Website: https://katieberry.ca

SHOPPING LINKS

CLAW: A Canadian Thriller:
Amazon eBook: https://amzn.to/31QCw7x
Paperback Version: https://amzn.to/31RYPK7
Amazon Audible Audiobook: https://amzn.to/2Gj3j45
(Also available on all other major audiobook platforms)

CLAW Resurgence:
Amazon eBook: https://amzn.to/2YeDdZt
Paperback Version: https://amzn.to/31RYPK7
Amazon Audible Audiobook: https://amzn.to/36nLSgk
(Also available on all other major audiobook platforms)

CLAW Emergence: Tales from Lawless – Kitty Welch:
Amazon eBook: https://amzn.to/37aSnAn
Large Print Paperback Version: https://amzn.to/3tTs0a9
Audiobook on Audible: https://amzn.to/3szAmXM

CLAW Emergence: Tales from Lawless – Caleb Cantrill:
Amazon eBook: https://amzn.to/3ldY0C3
Large Print Paperback Version: https://amzn.to/3meDVg9
Audiobook on Audible: https://amzn.to/3qkKvUe

CLAW Emergence Book 1: From the Shadows:
Amazon eBook: https://amzn.to/3VnB6di
Paperback Version: https://amzn.to/3Xjv5Q1
Audiobook: https://amzn.to/3TSvDyh
(Also available on all other major audiobook platforms)

CLAW Emergence Book 2: Into Daylight:
Amazon eBook: https://amzn.to/3JEC9Tf
Paperback Version: https://amzn.to/3NwKfhG
Audiobook Version: https://amzn.to/41y2lGR
(Also available on all other major audiobook platforms)

CLAW Emergence Book 3: Return to Darkness:
Amazon eBook: https://amzn.to/3GUVe1B
Paperback Version: https://amzn.to/47mrhCn
Audiobook Version: Coming Soon
(Also available on all other major audiobook platforms)

ABANDONED: A Lively Deadmarsh Novel Book 1 – Arrivals and Awakenings:
Amazon eBook: https://amzn.to/3jM3GDX
Paperback: https://amzn.to/3yruNLL
Audiobook: https://amzn.to/3yNot00
(Also available on all other major audiobook platforms)

ABANDONED: A Lively Deadmarsh Novel Book 2 – Beginnings and Betrayals:
Amazon eBook: https://amzn.to/3BTn4a9
Paperback: https://amzn.to/3BTneyh
Audiobook: https://amzn.to/3FrwcVF
(Also available on all other major audiobook platforms)

ABANDONED: A Lively Deadmarsh Novel Book 3 – Chaos and Corruption:
Amazon eBook: https://amzn.to/3HpBNMM
Paperback: https://amzn.to/3IOGTE7
Audiobook: https://amzn.to/3PtVyqr
(Also available on all other major audiobook platforms)

ABANDONED: A Lively Deadmarsh Novel Book 4 – Deception and Deliverance:
Amazon eBook: https://amzn.to/3wo6XqF
Paperback: https://amzn.to/3Qh5t3m
Audiobook: https://amzn.to/3NVOdC9
(Also available on all other major audiobook platforms)

Printed in Dunstable, United Kingdom